KNOCKED UP BY
THE DOM

PENELOPE BLOOM

1

KYLIE

I wait in line at the airport with a small bag that bulges at the seams. The woman in front of me gives it a curious glance, then does a double take when she sees I'm wearing a thin white dress with a bikini beneath. She makes an indelicate snort of disapproval through her nose and turns away.

Let her huff and puff. I'm going on this freaking vacation because I've earned it.I'm not even going to stop at a hotel before I go to the beach when I get there, even if I have to march straight off the plane by foot to the nearest ocean. So *yes, cranky lady*, I am wearing my bathing suit at the airport. Get over it.

For all my tough internal talk, her look still makes me feel a little self-conscious. I hug the bag a little tighter to my chest before unzipping a pocket on the side and pulling a crumpled post-card free. I look at it for probably the millionth time. It shows a scene of water so perfectly blue it's hard to tell where the sky ends, a rocky outcropping that makes a small cove where the water is clear enough to show the yellow sand beneath.

Blue skies and sandy beaches. That's what I need. Anything to get me a breather from the day-to-day grind of waking up for work, sitting at my desk for nine hours while I try to cling to what's left of my sanity, then feeling like my evening goes by in the blink of an eye.

I push the picture back down, closing my eyes and biting my lip. Bermuda. It has taken me months and months to save the money for the plane ticket and the place I'm staying at, not to mention the strings I had to pull to actually get a week off. It's all going to be worth it. Every second of it.

Someone bumps me from behind, knocking me off balance so I nearly drop my bag.

"Line's moving," says a man with a sweaty brow and beady black eyes.

I clear my throat, shuffling forward to take my place in front of the attendant, who asks to see my ticket.

She's a young girl, maybe in her mid twenties with a pixie haircut and upturned nose. She smacks her gum idly as she glances at my ticket, then the computer screen, and once more at my ticket.

"Is everything okay?" I ask.

She makes an attempt at looking regretful, but falls just short. "Looks like your flight was canceled. Next one is tomorrow afternoon, but that flight is overbooked, so you'd have to upgrade your to first-class. It'd be about eight hundred dollars for the upgrade."

Something deep inside me breaks. I feel it snap like an old, dry twig. A frigid cold spreads from the spot, numbing my stomach and then my whole chest. *Eight hundred dollars.* More than twice what I had to save for the ticket in the first place. Almost as much as it's going to cost to stay for the entire week.

"There has to be some other way," I say, trying not to let the panic I feel reach my voice. My hand on the counter shakes violently so I pull it back, gripping my bag to keep it still. "Please," I say.

She licks her lips and looks at the computer again. I watch her fingers tap away and her mouth press together in concentration.

"Well, there will be another flight in three days. I could have your ticket transferred to that flight for no cost."

"My vacation time is already arranged through work, I can't change it now," I say. "It has to be today. Tomorrow at the latest. I wouldn't have time to--it just has to be by tomorrow."

Someone behind me makes an annoyed sound. I glance over my shoulder to see the guy with the beady eyes who bumped me. His arms are crossed and he's tapping his foot dramatically. I ignore him, but the girl helping me glances at him and tenses a little.

"Ma'am," she says a little more curtly. "I'm sorry for the inconvenience, but there's nothing else I can do. Do you want me to upgrade you to first-class for tomorrow or transfer your ticket?"

"No," I say. "I want a refund." The words come out of me slowly and painfully. It's not the end of the world, though. I can just wait a few more months until another opportunity to get time off comes. I'm sure I can get my deposit back from the hotel.

The girl makes an obnoxiously placating face. "We unfortunately don't offer refunds in this case."

"This case?" I say, feeling my temper start to falter.

The man behind me clears his throat again.

"Need a cough drop, asshole?" I snap, turning at him with a look on my face that must be terrifying, because he flinches back.

The girl's eyes are wide now and her body is rigid. I know I'll feel guilty for this later, but right now I just feel the crushing disappointment numbing me to everything, even the stupidity of taking my anger out on this poor girl.

"You mean this case where you guys took my money weeks ago and now you're telling me I can't get what I paid for, but I also can't get my money back? You mean that case?"

"There's nothing I can do," says the girl robotically.

I sigh, feeling all the anger drain out of me as suddenly as it came. "It's fine. It's not your fault," I say. "I'll figure something else out. Just put it on hold for now, okay?"

She nods, shifting her eyes to motion for the next in line to come to the counter.

I turn and walk away from the counter and find a bench to sit on. I curl my arms around the bag and hug it in my lap, resting my head on it like a big pillow and willing myself not to cry. There's no point sitting here feeling sorry for myself.

Yeah, I worked my ass off for this vacation. Yeah, none of this is fair. But I'm not the kind of girl who wallows in self-pity. I just can't seem to make myself get up yet, not now. I decide to allow myself to wallow for just a few minutes. At least taking a week off work means I have time to mope in the airport for a little while. I don't let a single tear come, though I could cry a million in frustration and disappointment. I'm not going to cry over this. It's just a crushed dream I spent months looking forward to. It's only--

A deep voice draws my attention.

"Canceled?" asks the man.

My head pops up so I can see the speaker, but his back is to me. He wears a suit that looks expensive, but my eyes go straight past the material to the places where it hugs his fit body exceptionally well. Broad shoulders. Lean, athletic legs, and posture that says volumes about his confidence. His feet are wide, hands planted on the counter, and he leans in.

I listen to the girl tell him the same thing she told me, except this guy already had first-class tickets, so she tells him she can transfer his tickets over for tomorrow, no problem.

He sighs, turns away from the counter, and starts walking *directly toward me.*

I've heard the cliche before, but I think my heart actually stops when I see him coming for me. He's tall, with the most arrestingly blue eyes I've ever seen. A couple days' worth of scruff lines his crisp jawline and full lips. His hair is effortlessly pushed away from his face in a way that somehow speaks of rugged carelessness and yet polished at the same time. I've seen celebrities on the screen and magazines, but I've never seen a man so absolutely breathtaking in person before. Not even close.

He looks around the crowded benches, slowing a little as he scans for a place to sit. His eyes fall on me and I realize I'm not breathing, except right now I don't think I could even if I tried.

The corner of his mouth pulls up so slightly I think I might be imagining it. *Did he just smirk at me?*

I can't do anything but watch as this miracle of a man strides straight to the seat beside me and sits, giving me a full breath of his expensive cologne and something masculine and clean just beneath the scent. He practically towers over me, even sitting.

"Keep staring like you want to take a bite out of me and I might let you," he says in a smooth voice with a deep, gravelly undertone. The sound alone has me pressing my legs together to suppress the growing warmth and wetness dampening my bikini.

Of all the times in my life I had to be rebellious and wear a freaking bikini with a revealing cover-up to the airport, it had to be when Mr. Model decides to strike a conversation with me? And since when does the sight, *or sound*, for that matter, of a guy get me wet?

"Excuse me?" I ask weakly. My body finally shivers a little, taking in the air I've been denying it for too long, giving me no choice but to awkwardly sit there, sucking in air like I just jogged a few laps while he watches me with a sparkle of amusement in those intense blue eyes.

"The way you're looking at me," he says, reaching a hand out and placing a surprisingly gentle finger at my cheek and dragging it down to my jaw. The innocent touch explodes through me like it's electric until I feel breathless all over again. "Flushed cheeks. Slightly dilated pupils. Shortness of breath," he notes, taking a longer-than-necessary look at my rising and falling chest. "You're aroused," he says simply.

I close my mouth, unable to look in his eyes. Of course I'm freaking aroused, asshole. Not that I'm going to admit that to him, not now. "I... I don't..." I stammer, searching for any words that don't betray how desperately I want him to put those strong hands back on me, whether that's crazy or not.

"Your flight was canceled too. I was behind you in line," he explains. "So we both have twenty-four hours to kill."

I wait for him to say more, but he doesn't. He waits, watching me with those eyes, those analyzing, piercing eyes that I'm suddenly sure see straight through me. I can say whatever untruths I want, but this man knows. He knows how he's affecting me. As much as I hate to admit it, even the logical part of my brain is betraying me. After all, I *do* have the week off work, so it's not like I have anywhere to be. Why pass this up--whatever *this* is.

"There's a conference room," he says, guiding my eyes with his index finger to a hallway of closed doors. "Second one on the left. It's unlocked."

Without another word, he stands, brushes the wrinkles from his pants, and heads toward the hallway.

I watch after him, mouth hanging open. I look around, half-expecting to see grinning faces watching because I'm part of some cruel prank. I only see bored people waiting for flights with expressionless faces lit by phone screens.

I stand, still holding my bag close to my chest. To my right, I can see the doors that lead out of the airport, back to my little red car with a dent on the fender that someone kindly left me in a parking lot while I was getting groceries. My car, that will take me back to my humdrum little hamster wheel life, where I'll keep plugging in hour after hour so that maybe my year of work can buy me a few days of happiness. But that door is also safe. I know what happens if I walk through it. I'll listen to the radio on the way home, maybe pick up a gallon of ice cream and some wine, and I'll try to make the best of my week off from work, even if it's not in Bermuda.

To my left...

That door scares the hell out of me. I hear the distant click as he pulls it closed behind him and I wonder how long he'll wait for me. To a guy like him, casual sex probably is no big deal. He probably just wants to go through the motions, pass a little time, and then never see me again. Me though? I've never slept with a guy if I didn't think there was a good chance our relationship was going somewhere, but I've been left dissatisfied every time. The sex has been uninspiring and the conversation equally bad.

Between guys who can't last more than a few minutes and the ones whose idea of foreplay is digging around my vagina with their fingers like they're looking for spare change, I haven't had a whole lot of motivation to get back into dating lately.

The man waiting inside that conference room struck me as a profoundly different breed than any man I've ever been with before. The calmness and surety of his movements radiated confidence and experience. The way he read my body so clearly makes me think he'd know exactly how to satisfy me.

I realize I've started walking toward the exit, hands squeezing even tighter around my bag. It's so easy. Just one step after another and all the uncertainty and fear I feel about that door to the conference room gets farther and farther away. Every step takes me closer to the comfortable, if depressingly boring, life I'm used to. I can go back to my old life and suffocate on comfort and routine just as easily as taking a few more steps. Or...

The warm air rushes against my face when the automatic doors open, but I pause at the threshold. Somehow I know if I make that final step from the airport to outside, I'll never turn back. It could become another disappointment to add to this ruined vacation.

I put my hand on the glass beside the door before turning to take one last look toward the hallway where the man is waiting. A woman brushes past me irritably, trying to make her way outside. I watch her go. Like me, she's probably on her way home to steal a few hours of idle entertainment before diving back into the rat race.

I suck in a deep breath and turn back toward the hallway with the conference rooms. My heart beats violently and I can't seem to catch my breath, but I keep moving, knowing I can't stop or my resolve will crumble.

I'm going to do this. Whatever this is, I'm going to do it.

I'm standing outside the conference room door before I know it, hand hovering over the doorknob. I feel like my knees might give out, like every nerve in my body is screaming that this is crazy and I should turn and run as fast as I can. He could be a pervert, hell, he could even be a serial killer. But as nonsensical as it is, I can't picture it from him. Looking like he does, I can't see why he'd need to use any tricks to get what he wants from women.

I laugh a little at myself as I stand outside the door, realizing I'm probably one of a hundred to fall into his seductive trap, but knowing doesn't stop the pounding need to open that door.

I turn the knob and step inside.

2

DAMIAN

The door creaks open so slowly I can practically taste how nervous she is, and there's no sweeter fucking taste on the planet. I knew I had to have her as soon as I saw her. I have a lease with the airport to keep one of my personal planes here out of convenience, so it was a miracle I even happened to look toward the line of people waiting to check their bags and tickets.

But there she was. Wearing a bikini and a cover-up in the middle of an airport. Her chestnut hair and big brown doe eyes captivated me almost as much as her barely covered curves. She practically has innocence and inexperience written all over her. Something about the way she could pass for a hot-as-hell preacher's daughter combined with those unbelievable tits and perfectly tight ass has my cock so hard it hurts. One look and I know no man has given her the kind of orgasms she deserves--the kind of *treatment* she deserves.

That's about to change.

She steps inside hesitantly with wide eyes that dart around the room, skimming over every detail but always bouncing back to me--to my face, my chest, *my cock*.

Dirty girl.

A predatory smirk pulls at my mouth. I can't help feeling like I've just lured something pure and sweet into the darkness of my world, and maybe I have, but she's going to love every second of it.

She clears her throat. "I don't even know your name," she says with a nervous laugh that sounds like something between a squeak and a cough.

"Damian."

She swallows visibly. "I'm Kylie." She takes a couple steps toward me and extends her hand.

A handshake? I would laugh if the gesture didn't seem to perfectly fit the awkward and innocent image I'm already forming of this woman, and something about the simpleness of it is turning me on even more.

I reach to swallow her small hand up in mine, enjoying the smooth silkiness of her skin against my own rough touch.

"Do you come here often?" she asks, pulling back from the handshake and tugging at her dress, which is deliciously see-through and gives me a clear view of the black bikini she wears beneath.

"To this conference room?" I ask.

Her cheeks flush red. "To the airport?" She laughs a little at herself, shaking her head and taking a half-step back toward the door. "I'm sorry. This is completely crazy. I don't even know what I'm doing here, I should just--"

I move toward her, not touching her exactly, but with such urgency that she has no choice but to move back until she's against the wall and I'm in front of her, palms pressed to the wall on either side of her head. "Don't leave," I say.

Her chest is heaving, but the way her eyes lock on mine and her lips flush with red tells me it's not entirely from fear. She wants this, at least on some level, but she's never done something like it before. She needs an excuse--she needs me to take the responsibility so she won't feel guilty or ashamed.

I kiss her then, so forcefully at first that her head bangs into the wall a little with a dull thump. She moans in surprise against my lips, but wastes no time slipping her sweet, hot little tongue between my lips. It's not a hesitant kiss like most first kisses tend to be. It's not soft or tender. It's hungry. It's lust, hunger, and the sense of urgency all transformed into a frenzy. Her hands are stiff at first, but when I press my palm to her thigh and climb until the top of my fingers graze her pussy through her bikini, which is already warm and soaked through from her arousal, she awakens, digging her fingers into my back and exploring me as quickly as she can.

"I can't," she gasps between kisses, but her hands never stop. "This is crazy."

I push her back against the wall, gripping the base of her throat carefully--I know where to put pressure to give the illusion of danger without obstructing the airways in the slightest. A more experienced woman would want to feel the real danger of her air supply dwindling, but to her, I'm sure even the slightest implication will more than do the trick.

Surprise and fear register in her expression, but when she sees me lift my fingers that are wet from her sweet juices to my mouth and lick them clean, a moan of pleasure escapes her lips.

"You can't?" I ask. "Well *I can't* have you slipping away on me. Stay right there, Kitten," I add, before turning to the computer set up on the conference desk and yanking a few cords free. She's right where I left her when I come back, and her obedience already has me near the edge of my limits.

"Why is your dress still on?" I ask.

She gulps again, fingers twitching toward the hem of her dress but no more than that. "Y-you want me to take it off?" she asks. Her eyes dart to the door and she closes her fingers tightly around the fabric of her dress, her whole body tense.

"No one will disturb us," I say, stepping close enough to smell her arousal. She smells so sweet and pure that I can barely wait to taste her pussy, which I know will be incredible. "Take off your dress," I demand.

She doesn't move immediately, so I snap the cords between my fists, making a sound that sends her jumping. "Off. All of it."

I watch her closely. Her body language tells me everything I need to know. Clenched fists and slightly hunched posture both speak of apprehension, but there's no denying the hardened nubs of her nipples, the flush in her cheeks, her dilated pupils, and the way she's already wet as hell for me. She wants this as much as I do, and I'm not going to sacrifice the thrill for her by asking permission. Fuck that.

With slow, shaking hands, she pulls her dress up over her head and drops it beside her feet. I take her in, sucking in a shuddering breath as my eyes feast on the swell of milky soft skin of her tits and the way I can see the patch of wetness even against the black fabric of her bikini bottom. It takes everything in me not to go to her now and tear her clothes free with my hands or teeth--whichever comes first.

But I wait.

Her eyes meet mine and for several long moments nothing happens. Her innocent brown eyes transfixed by my icy blues. Her chest rises rapidly, breasts rising and falling hypnotically. My own breathing coming ragged now with my insatiable need to have her--to have every last fucking inch of her all to myself.

I've never needed to fuck a woman this badly, not even close.

She bites her full bottom lip, holding it there with her teeth while she reaches to untie her top. She frees those perfect tits, and goddamn, putting them away in the first place was a crime. She smiles shyly but with a hint of pride at my obvious admiration. Each breast falls down with a satisfying weight, and it's all I can take. I can't wait another fucking second to put my hands on her.

I rush forward, taking both her wrists and pressing them to the wall over her head. I quickly wrap the cord around them and then tie it off to an exposed pipe above her. She watches me carefully, but gives no resistance. *Dirty little kitten. You want this so fucking bad, don't you?*

I grip one of her breasts now that I have her where I want her, running my thumb over the hardened nub of her nipple. Goosebumps rise across her chest and arms.

"Very responsive to touch," I note. "That's good. But I'll have to be careful not to make you cum *too* fast."

"What if I say no?" she whispers.

The heat and sweetness of her breath brushes my face. I breathe it in, barely in control anymore. Nearly to the point that the only thing I can stand to do is turn her around and fuck her until she's full of my cum and can't think straight, until her knees are so weak I'll have to carry her out of here like the conquest she'll be.

"If you say no?" I ask. "There's only one way to find out."

3

KYLIE

He looms over me, never taking his hands from my body or that smoldering gaze from my eyes. He's all-consuming, all-powerful, and might as well be sexuality in the flesh as far as my body is concerned. His hands are like conduits that send my nerves into overdrive until even the slightest touch or sensation feels like it could bring me to my knees--but that won't happen as long as I'm tied and at his mercy.

God. What am I doing?

The small voice of reason breaks through my lust for a fraction of a second, but there's no way I'm stopping this now. I'm too far in. I've breathed the perfume of his attraction too deeply to stop now, maybe ever.

I should feel exposed and embarrassed, but I don't. I only feel the exhilaration of living outside the lines for what might be the first time in my life. I may have asked him what would happen if I said no, but I think a dirty part of me just wanted to hear him say it didn't matter what I said. I wanted to know he wanted me so badly that he wasn't going to let me walk out of here, no matter what.

But that's crazy. He's just trying to keep me on edge to

heighten the experience. That's all. Then again, maybe this is real. Maybe he decided walking into this room was consent enough and I was his as soon as I did.

His.

The word sends a shiver of excitement down my spine that explodes into warmth between my legs, soaking my already wet bikini bottoms until I'm more wet than I've ever been in my life.

I wait. I could tell him I want this. I could relieve the pressure and the unanswered question that hangs in the air, but to do that feels like it would be a crime. This is his world. I was lucky enough to stumble into it, and I'm not about to squander the experience.

His lips twist into an amused smile. "You want to play hard to get, Kitten?" he asks.

I feel a rush when he uses the pet name again. The possessiveness of it lights a fire in my stomach that has my pussy throbbing. I want to be his. His kitten. His plaything. His *anything.* I don't care if it's crazy to want all that from a stranger.

"I..." I breathe. It feels like all the air has left my lungs, like I can barely push out a word, let alone a sentence. "Are you sure you have the... right girl?" I ask.

He watches me for a long moment before responding, lips curling into a slow, amused grin. He leans in close, lips so close to my ear I can feel the heat of his breath and the tickle of his skin against mine. "I'm sure about one thing. Your fucking hands are tied, and you're not going anywhere until I've had my fun with you."

My knees go weak, and if it wasn't for the cords holding me from above, I would collapse. This isn't real. This *can't* be real. "Why me?" Is all I can manage.

"Because I knew I had to have you as soon as I saw you." When he steps back I see he has complete control. His face is calm and he watches me with those gorgeous, startling eyes. "It's just too bad I don't have all the right tools at my disposal." He takes a look around the room with real regret.

"Tools?" I ask.

He shrugs. "Paddles, hot wax, ice... maybe even a spanking bench would do nicely. Then there's always the Saint Andrew's cross, a personal favorite."

He's watching me closely, studying my reaction to each word. I wonder how much he can really be learning, because even I don't know how I feel about all that.

"Don't worry, Kitten. You'll still cum so hard you'll be screaming. We'll probably have airport security in here before we're done."

"I've never been loud," I blurt, and I feel my cheeks burning red hot from embarrassment. "In bed, I mean... Not that I've been in bed often--well, it's not like I don't know what I'm doing." My hands itch to cover my face even though I can't move them, or better yet plug my stupid mouth from digging myself into a deeper of hole. *Perfect.* Just when he was convinced he wanted to sleep with me, I go and show him what a social klutz I am.

But the sense of sexual hunger he practically drips only seems to grows stronger. "You've never been loud, have you? Then you've clearly never been treated right."

His fingers slowly move to his buttons, which he carelessly pops open one by one to reveal the most perfectly sculpted torso I've ever laid eyes on. The heat between my legs becomes so intense that I shift a little uncomfortably from the ever growing wetness. When I look at the bulge in his slacks I can't help thinking he could slide in so effortlessly right now, even with a cock that size. And *God*, I don't know if I've ever felt so empty in my life, so ready to be filled, so hungry for the friction of skin against mine.

He flicks his belt buckle loose and undoes the button on his pants, letting my anticipation grow as I watch him step closer, taking in the line of hair running from his belly button and disappearing beneath his gray briefs that are just barely visible. When he finally pulls down his pants, there's a dark spot at the tip of his impressive bulge from pre-cum.

I lick my lips, unable to take my eyes from the shape of his cock struggling against the fabric of his briefs. He hooks his thumbs in the waistband and strips them down, letting his cock spring proudly free.

The sight of it literally takes the breath from my lungs. It's definitely the biggest I've ever seen, and I'm already imagining what it will feel like inside me. *How could I not be?*

"Now," he says, stepping up to me so his cock is pressed between us where it throbs, warm against my belly. He bends his neck to kiss my ear, tugging slightly with his lips. "You are not to speak or make a sound. Every time you moan or speak, I'll make you wait another ten seconds to have your orgasm. Am I clear?"

"Yes..." I say hesitantly. Rules? Why does the idea of rules have my skin tingling and my heart pounding with excitement.

"Yes, Sir," he corrects.

"Yes, Sir," I say.

He groans with satisfaction, bending to kiss my neck and roughly grip my tits. "That's fucking perfect."

My back arches against his touch and my eyes slam shut. Every little movement is an explosion, rocking me to my core and bringing the rush of the world's most premature orgasm closer and closer.

He surprises me by hooking his arms under my thighs and lifting me effortlessly onto his shoulders so my legs are spread in front of his face. I still wear my bikini bottoms, which is embarrassingly soaked by now, but he clearly doesn't care.

He runs the flat of his tongue slowly and languidly along my crease over the material, groaning with pleasure. "You taste so fucking sweet, Kitten. I knew you would."

I bite my lip hard and squeeze my hands tight around the cord holding my wrists together. Everything about him screams masculinity. He likes the way I *taste?* Jesus... Why is that so insanely hot?

Any thoughts of self-consciousness I might have had are quickly obliterated by the blinding need for more. More of him. More of his tongue. More of his filthy words. More everything.

I grind my hips into him, wincing when a moan spills from my lips.

He looks up at me, and the sight of his perfect face between my legs is one I'll never forget. "Ten seconds, Kitten. Naughty, naughty."

With any other guy, I'd be relieved that they weren't planning to hump me for ten seconds and then cum, only to roll off and fall asleep. But with Damian? The orgasm building inside me is like a flood ready to burst, and holding it back is almost torture. He has barely had his hands on me for more than a few minutes and I'm already so desperate to cum I could scream--but that would mean I'd have to wait another ten seconds.

He yanks on the waistband of my bikini, sliding it free and lifting my legs high enough to pull them past his head before lowering me back down. I'm completely naked now, and more than a little aware of the fact that we're in an unlocked conference room of a crowded airport. I can even hear what sounds like a young couple not far away complaining about their layover.

His mouth against my bare pussy is too much. Another moan escapes me, and I can't even clap my hand to my mouth to stifle the sound because the cords are still holding me hostage.

He makes a muffled sound with his lips pressed to my clit, and the vibration bursts through me like liquid ecstasy. I cry out again, distantly noticing the conversation outside the door falls silent, but I'm too far gone to care now.

Twenty more seconds.

My heels dig into his back, thighs scissoring tightly around his head so that I'm afraid I might be choking him, but I can't help it. It's everything I can do not to scream, to yank my hands free of these cords so I can rake my fingers roughly through his hair.

I start to hope he'll misjudge and give me the orgasm my body is begging for, but just when I can feel myself about to push over the edge, he stops, lowering me back to the ground. He turns me around, giving me a firm slap on the ass that stings but sends a shockwave of arousal through me, and then grips my hips.

"You didn't think I was going to let you cum before I got to feel that tight little pussy, did you?"

"No," I gasp.

"Ten seconds," he growls. "And it's no, Sir."

"No, Sir."

"Ten more seconds."

I grit my teeth, knowing it's unfair but also knowing there's no point debating with him. His word is absolute, just like his power over me.

I hold my breath as he lines up the head of his cock with my pussy. He presses into me, squeezing the first inch into me and stretching my walls to their limit. My cheek presses into the wall with the force of each thrust and his powerful hands grip me while he pulls me into him, using me like a fucktoy as he works inch after inch into me until I think there can't possibly be any more.

I finally feel the flat of his hips against my ass just as his cock presses so far into me I feel it pressing against my cervix. I gasp out another surprised moan, mentally chiding myself because I know he's keeping count, and he's going to enjoy dragging this out every second I give him an excuse to.

"You're so fucking tight, Kitten. I knew you would be."

I nearly respond to say something about how any woman would feel tight with a cock like his, but I've learned my lesson and I keep my lips pressed tightly together, still struggling to hold back the moans as he glides in and out of me. I'm so wet I can hear his every movement into me, but I know there's no need to feel embarrassed because I can sense his own arousal mounting. His breath is heavier now and his hands are squeezing me even tighter, hard enough I'll bruise. For some reason I love the thought of wearing his marks. He pounds into me so hard the sound of his hips against my ass must be audible even from the baggage claim.

Just when I know one more thrust will drive me over the edge and rip the orgasm from me that is waiting to burst, he stops.

"One... two... three," he starts counting.

I want to beg him for mercy, for the friction of his cock inside me, but I know speaking will only prolong his beautiful torture. I can't help myself from pressing my ass into him, seeking more of his length.

He chuckles. "Dirty little Kitten. You want to cum? Then you had better keep quiet this time."

I press my lips into the wall, hoping the pressure will be enough to keep me from crying out again, and I wait, struggling against his iron grip. He finally resumes his pace, pumping his cock into me with relentless rhythm, driving me into the wall with every thrust.

I can try all I want, but there's no stopping the sounds that come. I moan, I gasp, I curse, and I beg him for more. He stops keeping count, and I see the way his eyebrows draw down over those breathtaking eyes and I know he's as lost in this as I am.

He pounds into me and tenses just as my orgasm finally breaks free, tightening the walls of my pussy around his pulsing cock, milking his length for every drop of his hot cum. My whole body convulses and shakes. If not for his hands on my hips and the cords around my wrists I would crumple to the ground in a puddle of satisfied bliss.

"Fucking hell," he says. "I've never--"

The door swings open. A man wearing a security uniform stands at the door, eyes wide as he takes in the scene. Damian eases out of me shamelessly, and moves in front of my exposed body, blocking me from view of the security guard.

"Back out and close the fucking door if you want to keep your job. And if you so much as think about laying your eyes on her, I'll take more than your job."

A chill runs through me. The brutal way he talks to the man reminds me I know nothing about Damian, and yet here I stand with his cum running down my thighs. I should feel dirty and ashamed, but I don't. I feel alive. I feel more alive than I've ever felt.

To my surprise, the security guard closes the door, leaving us alone again. Damian reaches up to untie the cords and eases them off my wrists, taking great care to inspect where they left slight red marks on my skin from all the wiggling around I did. He makes a dissatisfied face. "Fuck. I don't even have any ointment for your skin."

"It's fine," I say a little awkwardly as I bend to find my clothes. I pick up my bikini, feel how soaked it is, and drop it back to the ground. I unzip my suitcase and about thirty swimsuits nearly burst out from how tightly I packed them all in.

Damian grins. I see he's sliding his briefs back on and looking for his pants. "That's all you packed? Swimsuits?"

I blush. "I was supposed to be going on vacation. To Bermuda."

"You still will," he says.

I frown, but the finality of his tone erases any doubt that he might be joking with me or lying. "You're serious?"

Damian brushes my cheek with his finger. "You bet that pretty little ass of yours I'm serious." He picks out a pink swimsuit and bends down, carefully lifting my ankle and sliding my foot through the opening. Once he pulls the bikini up to my hips, he takes his time circling me to make sure it's on properly.

I clear my throat. "I can dress myself, you know."

"I'll have to teach you not to mouth off to me like that. But that's a lesson for later. Maybe even tonight."

I try not to show the excitement his words fill me with. I didn't want to dwell on the idea, but somewhere deep down I knew this would be a one-off kind of thing. But he's talking about tonight?

And the way he carefully helps me get my clothes back on, finding every excuse he can to press his body to mine as he slips my top on--it's starting to make me think dangerous thoughts. *Stupid* thoughts.

Once he slides my cover-up on and does a final careful inspection, he finishes dressing himself. "Come with me. Stay close by my side, Kitten. Remember. You're mine now. If you stray, there will be consequences."

I bow my head, part of me unsure how to process everything and the other part wanting to jump headlong into whatever Damian is planning for me. The idea of being his--submitting to him--it calls to me so strongly I'm almost ready to throw everything away for this man I hardly know.

I follow him out into the hallway, back into the public eye. Every woman within a hundred feet of Damian perks up, glancing hopefully toward him like he's setting off some kind of instinctual sex radar. I gather as many glares as he does admiring looks, but the way he holds his hand on the small of my back makes it clear to everyone we pass that I'm his. *They don't have to know I've only known him for thirty minutes...*

A thousand questions burn on the tip of my tongue, but something in the way Damian holds himself makes me stay silent for now. It's not so much that I fear his anger. It's that I trust him to tell me what I need to know when I need to know it.

I should laugh at that. I'm putting more trust in a stranger than I would normally put in my best friend, but I can't help what I feel. There's a connection between us already, like something magnetic inside us snapped together the moment our eyes met.

He takes me through a small door near one of the boarding

tunnels, leading the way down a set of stairs that opens up to the runway. A warm breeze rustles my hair and the sound of airplane engines is suddenly overwhelming.

"Are we allowed to be here?" I ask.

He points to a small but luxurious airplane a few dozen yards off. "That one is mine. Come on."

"Why were you buying tickets to Bermuda if you have a personal plane?" I ask

His confidence falters for a moment, and somehow he's even sexier in his moment of vulnerability. "I guess you caught me. I wanted an excuse to talk to you."

"You don't strike me as the type of guy who needs to make excuses."

"Sometimes, no. But I wanted you so badly I didn't want to take any chances."

I blush. "You keep saying that and I might start to believe you."

"You had better believe me," he says, eyes igniting again with a hint of the fire I saw before. He kisses me, but it's not like the furiously, hungry kiss from the conference room. His lips brush mine tenderly now, almost lovingly. I kiss him back, until my body feels like it might melt into a puddle right here on the runway.

He pulls back with a cocky grin. "Easy. I'm all for exhibition-ism, but if you keep looking at me like that I'll have to fuck you right here, and I don't think even I could get us out of a night in a cell for that one."

I look away, embarrassed. "Maybe we should get on your plane, then."

He takes me toward the plane, where his pilot is already opening up a door that folds out into a staircase. Damian helps me up carefully, as if he's worried I might fall. Normally the kind of attention he's showing me would probably insult me, but there's something so sincere in his protectiveness that I can't seem to get enough.

The interior of the plane is more extravagant than I would've imagined. The carpet is plush and looks like it would feel amazing if I was barefoot. Polished wood paneling and even paintings adorn the walls. The main cabin is set up more like a living room than a commercial airliner, with a few comfortable looking single seats, a couch, a mini-bar, and even a fish tank lit from underneath to display an impressive collection of expensive looking fish.

"Aren't there weight limits on airplanes? Can you really have a *fish tank* and still fly?"

"This model is designed to hold at least sixty passengers. Keeping it under fifteen lets me have some luxuries."

I laugh. "So you chose a fish tank?"

He shrugs. "If I'm honest, I don't even pay attention to it all. In my line of work, extravagance inspires confidence from my clients. I show them what they want to see. No more, no less."

"What exactly do you do?" I ask.

"Sir," says a pretty young flight attendant who hurries in from the front cabin. I take her in from head to toe and an immediate, stabbing jealousy spikes through me.

Of course he'd have a beautiful flight attendant on his personal plane. He has probably slept with her, too. I push the thoughts away as soon as they come though. I didn't even know Damian an hour ago. I have no business even feeling a hint of jealousy over what he might have done before that. All I have a right to care about is how he acts going forward.

"What is it?" he snaps.

"Mr. Holland said to tell you there was a problem with the contract. He said you'd--"

"Damn it," growls Damian. He look to me regretfully, but seems to have already made up his mind over something. "Make sure she's comfortable." He leans in to kiss me again, but he's distracted and the kiss is little more than a peck. "I'll be as fast as I can. Wait here for me."

I watch him go, settling into the comfortable chair with a growing sense of unease. Being apart from Damian seems to break the spell. All the certainty I had that I wasn't being insane by sleeping with him and getting on a private jet with him is going up in smoke. I dig my fingers into the armrests of the chair.

"Would you like a drink?" asks the flight attendant.

"Yes, please. Something strong," I add.

She smiles and moves off toward the bar.

I look to the doorway when I hear footsteps coming up the stairs. But instead of Damian's imposing figure, it's a slim woman with an amazing body. She flashes a smile to the flight attendant, who looks extremely uncomfortable. "I didn't think he was expecting you," she says cautiously.

The woman glares. "Do you expect him to fill you in on every detail of his personal life? Scurry off, honey. I need to talk to her." Her eyes shift to me and I can't help squirming in my seat.

The woman clicks over in her expensive heels and sits across from me. Her smile is predatory. "I haven't had the pleasure of meeting you. Damian did say he'd bring some fresh meat for us to play with tonight, but you're not what I was expecting." She looks down her pert little nose at me, like I just fell out of a dumpster.

My stomach turns cold at her words. Fresh meat? "I'm sorry. Who are you?" I ask.

She purrs an obnoxious imitation of a laugh. "I'm Faleena. Damian's woman. His only *real* woman, despite whatever lies he filled your head with to get you this far."

I don't want to believe her, but all the doubt already swirling around my mind makes it impossible not to cling to what she's saying. "Why would he lie to me?"

"Oh, to be so naive again," she muses. "What a luxury." Faleena leans forward like she's about to let me in on a grand secret. "He told you what he had to so you'd come with him. He probably fucked you too, didn't he? Made you feel special?"

I can't meet her eyes. My fingers curl and uncurl on the hem of my dress. I feel like the dumbest woman in the world for falling into his trap, and right now I want nothing more than to leave, to never look back and pretend this was all a bad dream.

She throws her head back and laughs. "Of course he did. Well I hope you enjoyed your one-on-one time with him. I don't expect he'll be very interested in you past tonight. Only a real woman can keep his attention for long." Her voice lowers to a whisper. "I wouldn't blame you if you ran off. But if you're going to leave, you may not want to wait long. He won't let you go if he catches you."

I take my bag and push past her without a word, squeezing my eyes shut to hold back the tears of embarrassment. They come anyway. I knew it was too good to be true. I knew the perfect guy would never fall into my lap like that, but I still went along with it like an idiot.

What did I get for putting myself out there for once? For letting go and living a little? I get to look like a silly, stupid little girl. I feel like an even bigger fool when I remember the way he came inside me. At the time, I was so lost to his will that I didn't even consider the implications. I'm an idiot. I'm going to go home. Then I'm going to wait out the rest of my vacation time, and I'll go back to work. I'll move on and pretend none of this ever happened. It'll be a bad memory, and if I'm lucky, I can eventually push it so far from my mind it disappears.

Unless he got you pregnant. A nasty little voice says in my head. I scoff at the thought, shaking my head and wiping away the tears, already moving on from the self-pity stage and into the angry, resentful stage. What would be the chances of that? A guy like him probably had a vasectomy a long time ago so he could go around fucking whoever he wanted without protection like the animal he is. I should make an appointment to get tested. Lord only knows what kind of diseases the man could have.

A distant part of me questions whether I should believe the word of that catty bitch of a woman, maybe I'm latching onto the idea of his betrayal too quickly. It's almost an excuse that will let me go running back to my simple, predictable life. After all, it's one stranger's word over another. But what I was about to do was so far beyond my comfort zone, it only took the shadow of doubt to shatter my confidence. Running off that airplane was easier than walking into the conference room, and isn't that what I've always done? The easy thing. I don't know why it should surprise me that I'm doing what's easy now.

My thoughts leave an empty, painful pit in my stomach. On one hand, I believe the woman. Guys like him don't just come along to sweep girls up into some life of romance and passion. He could have any woman in the world, so of course she was telling the truth. Luring me onto that plane was just a game for him. I guess simply sleeping--no fucking, it was definitely fucking a woman isn't enough of a challenge for someone like him, he has to add humiliation and degradation to the mix.

Second by second, my confusion and doubt over running off the plane is solidifying into a single, overwhelming emotion. *Anger.* It's getting easier and easier to explain to myself how Faleena's words must have been true, and it's getting easier to picture Damian as some kind of monster instead of the man I thought he was.

I make it back inside the airport terminal, using a staircase like the one he led me down just a few minutes ago, but this time choosing a different entrance at random. Once I'm back upstairs, I look out the huge windows overlooking the runways and spot Damian striding back toward the private jet. He looks so big, even from up here. So imposing. So confident.

I set my jaw. *And so much like an asshole. Fuck you, Damian. I hope I never see you again.*

4

DAMIAN

My cock is already throbbing with the need to take her again when I climb the stairs back onto my private plane. Maybe I will. I'll just tell the staff to stay in the pilot's cabin so we can have some privacy. I bet my little kitten has never been fucked at ten thousand feet.

The grin on my face slips when I step into the cabin.

"What the fuck is she doing here?" I ask Jenny, my flight attendant, whose mouth is working silently, unable to come up with a response.

Faleena stands, smoothly pushing Jenny aside and answering for her. "I'm afraid I scared away your little plaything. I implied we were back together," she practically purrs.

"Where is Kylie?" I ask, ignoring Faleena and searching the cabin and then the pilot's cockpit.

"She left," says Jenny in a voice barely above a whisper.

"She left?" I roar. "She fucking left? You let her leave?"

Jenny's eyes well with tears, and despite my rage, I know I'm taking my anger out on the wrong person. I grit my teeth, pushing out the closest thing to an apology I can manage. "It's okay. Go wait in the cockpit while I deal with *this*."

Faleena gives me an amused arch of her eyebrow. "Really? We're going to resort to name calling already? I guess I shouldn't be surprised. You always were just a brute in expensive suits."

"Fuck off. I need to go find her."

"She's long gone," Faleena says, stopping me at the door. "She left at least ten minutes ago. Judging by the way she stormed out of here crying like a baby, she's probably already in her car on the way home. But you two exchanged information, of course?" It's not a question. Faleena watches me with knowing eyes. "You wouldn't fuck someone without knowing more than their first name..." Her lips form a mocking pout. "Or would you?"

I look out over the runway, knowing how slim my chances are of finding her now. "What the fuck did you tell her?"

"Enough to make sure that cock of yours never goes near her again." She steps toward me, swaying her hips purposefully and pulling her shoulders back to expose her cleavage. "Because I want it all to myself again."

The anger that rises inside me is so hot and unstable that I have to hold an open palm up to stop her from coming any closer. I've never laid my hands on a woman in a way that wasn't meant to bring pleasure, but I swear to God, if Faleena takes another step toward me right now... I don't know if I'll be able to stop myself.

"Get the fuck off my plane. Get the fuck out of my life. I never want to see your face again. Do you understand me? You're dead to me." I thought she already *was* dead to me when I broke things off a few months ago. Like all the relationships before, I didn't let it go on for long. Every woman until Kylie has felt like an empty husk compared to her. Scratch the surface and there's nothing of meaning inside, nothing for me to hold on to. Not Kylie though... It sounds crazy, but I just instinctively know that she's meant to be mine. And now she's God knows where because of this fucking bitch.

Faleena's confidence finally slips. Her eyebrows pull down in confusion. "You'd throw me away for that little girl? She can't handle you, Damian. Not like I can. She's not worth your time."

"Out," I say quietly, already feeling the loss settling into my chest like something black and putrid knowing the feeling will fester. Not worth my time? I've never felt anything like I felt when I was with her. I knew I didn't need dates. I didn't need to know her favorite color or her zodiac sign or what her childhood was like. I felt the connection between us on such a pure, primal level that there was no question.

She is the one, and now she might be gone forever. I know my chances are slim, but I'm not going to stop looking for her until I find her again. The thought of her out there right now thinking I used her is eating a fucking hole in my chest, and worse--the thought that I might never see her again is too much. I don't care how long it takes. I'm going to find her.

5

KYLIE

Three Years Later

~

The sound of keys clicking on keyboards fills the stale office space until the air conditioner, which is directly over my cubicle, kicks on. I lean back in my chair, cracking my neck and trying to stretch my sore shoulders. A spreadsheet stares back at me full of billing figures from the hospital's clients. Thanks to a massive system crash, we're having to re-enter the last two years of data. *Manually*.

Today is the fourth day we've been on what Steve, my manager, likes to call "Defcon Four." Apparently, Defcon Four means he can force us all to work overtime without paying us overtime. I'm still trying to figure that one out, but not too hard, because I'm sure the answer is something along the lines of "because you all need this job too badly to do anything about it".

Unfortunately, that's very true.

Melina scoots her chair over from the cubicle beside mine, bumping playfully into me. She waggles her eyebrows. "Steve had Indian for lunch. And he just went to the bathroom across the hall."

I roll my eyes and grin, even though it's hard to feel anything but bitterness right now. The bathroom across the hall is the one Steve goes to when he needs some privacy for an extended bathroom stay. As gross as it sounds, we all keep an eye out for his daily visit, because it means we get thirty minutes to slack off in what is normally a day of micro-managing and whip-cracking.

But when he has Indian food, it's practically a day off.

"How's your work coming?" I ask.

She blows out a dismissive puff of air. "You know? Sometimes I think pretending to work is harder than the real thing."

I shake my head, laughing. "You're unbelievable. You know we're all stuck here until this data gets in the system, right? What is it you're doing that's so important you want to keep us in 'Defcon Four' status any longer than we have to be?"

"Roll on over," she says, yanking my chair over to her cubicle by force. She switches to a tab on her internet browser with search results for masquerade style costumes. "I need help picking."

"For what? Are you filming your own version of *Eyes Wide Shut* or something?"

She gives me an unimpressed look. "No. I'm going to a fancy shmancy party tonight because Alec is taking me."

Alec is her latest boyfriend. Like every guy she dates, he's obnoxiously wealthy and handsome. I still haven't quite figured out what bootleg version of Tinder she has where all the guys have six figure incomes, but she must have some secret beyond big boobs and a pretty face.

I raise my hands, shaking them around and making a "woo-OoOo" noise.

She slaps at me. "You're just jealous. But you shouldn't be, because I'm bringing you as our plus one."

"Unless it's a plus one and a half, you had better find someone else. My sitter can't watch Dean tonight."

"Already taken care of. Alec arranged for a professional nanny to come watch him. Any other excuses? Go ahead, try me. I've covered all the usual bases, Kylie. You're not weaseling your way out of this one."

"I need sleep," I say. "This schedule is killing me, and Dean is waking up all hours of the night lately--"

"Alec got the nanny through the whole week. She'll be at your disposal for the next *seven days*. That's seven days of as much nappage and sleeping in as you can handle. Only if you go with me tonight, though," she adds with a wicked little smile.

"Tonight? Seriously? What do you plan to do, get four hour shipping on your order?" I ask, nodding to the screen.

"Nope," she says. "In-store pickup, smartass. And if you don't pick something out for yourself, I'm going to pick for you. *And it's going to be slutty as hell if you let me pick.*"

I give her a long, scathing look, in some ways hoping she'll relent, but she's not budging. I can see it from the stubborn set of her jaw. "Why me?" I groan, reaching for the mouse to click through the masks, dresses, and heels.

"Because you need some social interaction. I know you're a single mom and it's not easy to get out, but I'm taking that out of the equation this time. You're too young to swear off men. I don't care what Dean's dad did to you. You need a rebound fuck, because God knows you haven't touched a man in years."

"Says who?" I ask, more than a little defensively. I've also never talked to her about Dean's father. I haven't talked to anyone about him. Just the thought of it brings up the memory of Damian's piercing blue eyes and the way he touched me, the sounds of my moans cutting through the quiet conference room.

It's a memory that still fills me with the darkest, most shameful kind of arousal there is, because if I ever see Damian again, I think I'll throw something at him. Something heavy.

She gives me her best side eyes.

I sigh. "Even if that's true, do you really expect me to go to this party and just... *fuck* some stranger?" *Been there, done that,* I think with more than a little bitterness. It has been years since I let Damian take me in that conference room and knock me up. Years since the painful realization that he was just taking advantage of me. But the wound still feels as fresh as if it were yesterday. Time has done nothing to dull the pain. If anything, I feel more angry now than I was back then.

As much as I hate Damian for the way he used me, at least I got my baby boy out of it. When I found out I was pregnant, it felt like the end of the world. A stranger's baby was in my belly, and I knew I'd never tell him, not in a million years, not that I even knew how to contact him. Maybe that was selfish of me. I don't know anymore, but before long the baby didn't feel like it was his to know about. He was mine. Little Dean was mine. I carried him in my belly all those months. I gave birth all by myself in the hospital and suffered the concerned looks of the nurses and doctors. I endured the judgmental looks from people in the lobby when they wheeled me out alone with my baby boy. And I've been raising him by myself since the day he was born and we are doing just fine.

Would Damian have helped if he knew? Maybe. I can't fault him for not helping when he doesn't even know about Dean, but I couldn't risk it. If he was anything like Faleena said, there was the very real possibility he'd somehow decide to start a legal battle and steal Dean from me. No matter how small the risk might have been, I couldn't take that kind of chance.

"Earth to Kylie," says Melina. "You're thinking about it again, aren't you?"

"Let's just pick out this stupid dress so I can get tonight over with."

She claps her hands together and smiles. "That's the spirit!"

I SIT in the back of Alec's car wearing the lacy white dress and extravagant mask I picked out. I have to admit, it was fun getting dressed up for this, even if I think I'll probably end up standing in a corner somewhere. But there's something about having a mask covering most of my face that gives me a thrilling sense of anonymity, like I could leave the real Kylie behind just for tonight and be someone else, someone who isn't damaged goods carrying around luggage to spare.

Melina's dress and mask are black, while Alec wears a perfectly fitted suit and a simple black mask to cover his face.

"Thank you, by the way," I say to Alec. "It was really nice of you to pay for Dean's sitter."

He waves his hand dismissively. "Don't even mention it. No offense, but I'd do anything to make my little minx happy," he says, gripping Melina's knee.

We join a small convoy of ridiculously expensive looking cars--all glossy and cleaned to perfection. We drive through a wrought iron gate with an embellished "P" in the center. The path leading to the house is a winding trail that cuts through tall bushes and eventually weaves through a green, pristine field lit by so many floodlights that I can't even see the stars overhead.

The house itself is bigger than a hotel. Countless windows twinkle across the slopes and curves of its exterior. Beautifully crafted balconies and trellises adorn the upper floors of the house, giving it an almost medieval look that makes me feel like I'm about to step into a castle.

A valet takes Alec's keys admiring the car. Alec is kind enough to help me from the car once Melina is out and straightening her dress.

"Thank you," I mutter distractedly as I take in the house and the crowd of black-clad party goers making their way inside, many of whom are openly staring at my white costume. *Every-body* is wearing black. From a single glance, it's painfully clear this party was supposed to be a *black* masquerade party, and my sweet, infuriating friend failed to mention that to me.

"You didn't tell me to pick something black," I hiss to Melina.

She winces. "Sorry! I skimmed the invitation. I didn't know either. I just happened to pick black."

I cross my arms, looking toward the car, wondering if it's too late to escape. Showing up to a stranger's party is bad enough, but being the only one wearing white? They'll be offering my body up to science so they can study the first recorded case of death by embarrassment. "I can't," I say.

"It's fine," says Alec. "It's just a theme. There will probably be others who didn't read the rules or who outright ignored them."

"Yeah. Besides, I can totally find someone your size and drug her. We can steal her dress and stuff her in a closet somewhere."

"Charming," says Alec dryly.

She shoots him a look full of daggers. "If I want to drug someone and steal their clothes to help my friend, I will."

Alec seems to already know better than to make a point of arguing with Melina, because he takes her by the arm and motions toward the front entrance. "Shall we?"

I follow beside Melina, giving myself an endless inner pep-talk about how it doesn't matter if people are looking at me like I'm an attention-seeker. I'll probably never see them again anyway, so who cares what they think. Right?

Once we're inside, I'm distracted by the scale of the house. Two winding staircases lead to an upper level that overlooks the grand entrance. Men and women are already mingling upstairs, while even more are moving through the huge space downstairs. Waiters and waitresses circulate the room with platters of drinks and hors d'oeuvres. A deep, pulsing music plays throughout the room from unseen speakers, and in a few spaces I see women dancing against men and even a pair who are making out at the far end of what might be the living room.

I take in a sharp breath, feeling even more out of place than I did when I realized I got the dress code wrong. "What do I do?" I ask Melina.

"Mingle!" She says cheerily. "You've got a mask on, girl. Reinvent yourself for the night. Go wild. No consequences. Just enjoy it."

And like a true friend, Melina strolls off with Alec, leaving me cluelessly looking around the room. It's not long before a tall man with narrow shoulders and a cleft chin approaches me. "Beautiful," he says.

I smile self-consciously, tucking a hair behind my ear. I can't see much of him except that he has short, somewhat curly hair and nice teeth. "Thank you, I--"

"Leave," says a man with a simple black mask and tailored suit, who is a few inches taller and much broader in the shoulders than the man I was talking to.

It looks like there's about to be an altercation, but the first man backs away with a sour expression when he sees how much bigger the other man is.

I look up at the stranger, feeling the oddest tingle of recognition, but I can't place it. "That was rude," I say.

I realize his chest is heaving with heavy breaths. He breathes deeply through his nose before he speaks. "Come with me."

"I probably shouldn't--I'm here with a friend. She'll be--"

"I won't ask again," he says.

Something in his tone stops me short. I swallow hard, feeling the familiarity grow even more now. No man has talked to me like this before, except once... Even though my brain is telling me to leave, to just walk outside and never look back, my body moves to follow him.

He takes me past the main section of the party, back through hallways that grow less and less crowded with every step we take. We eventually reach a thick wooden door at the bottom of a short staircase. He turns the knob and opens the door to reveal a completely separate party area, except everyone here wears red.

Even the walls are a deep, blood red with dark wood paneling. The music is slower, but with a more pulsating beat that feels sensual and mysterious.

I nearly fall backwards when a woman passes us wearing nothing but a red thong and mask. Her impressive breasts bounce with each step, and she takes her time slowing in front of my mysterious stranger, pouting a little when he doesn't seem to return her interest.

"Where are we?" I ask.

He turns suddenly, pressing me to the wall with a firm hand so I'm forced to look into his startling blue eyes. "If you trust me, I'll open up a world you've never known, a hunger you didn't know you had."

I open my mouth to speak but can't seem to find words that make sense. "Why should I trust you? I don't even know you." Or do I? Every second I spend in his presence makes the strange feeling of recognition grow stronger and stronger until I feel like realization is on the tip of my tongue.

"You could leave, but then you'd wonder what you walked away from," he says smoothly.

It's impossible not to feel drunk on the air in this place, like the throbbing beat is pushing its way into my lungs and making my pulse match the slow rhythm, like I can't breathe anything but his enticing scent, which is also oddly familiar.

"Do I know you?" I ask again.

"I could tell you, but that would ruin the fun, wouldn't it?"

"I don't know if fun is the word I'd--" I yelp as he sweeps me away from the wall by my waist, gripping me and parading me through the crowded space like I'm his property.

Melina's words echo in my mind, reminding me to just let go, to enjoy this. Nothing bad is going to happen to me with so many people around. *Probably.* I follow him deeper into the room as we wind through an impossibly large space full of candlelit alcoves, dark rooms lit by black lights where half-naked men and women gyrate, and past what even looks like a full-blown torture chamber.

He finally opens a door at the end of a dimly lit hallway with an old-fashioned brass key. Inside, the music is nothing but a dull thumping I can only hear if I strain. The relative quiet is shocking--unnerving, even.

He reaches up to remove his mask. It feels like an ice-cold fist clutches my heart, squeezing until my arms and legs are tingling. *Damian.*

"No," I say. "No. No fucking way," I turn to the door, trying to pull it open.

He plants a hand on the door, keeping it shut. "Kylie," he says softly. "You have no idea how long I've been trying to find you."

"Yeah? You look like you're trying real hard while you were playing dress-up here."

His jaw flexes. "Kylie... I need you to hear me out. If you still want to leave once I've said what I need to say, you can."

"I can leave now if I want to," I growl stupidly, yanking on the door but I can't even make it budge.

"I know Faleena talked to you on the plane that day. She was *lying.* Everything she said was bullshit."

I shake my head, laughing humorlessly. "That's convenient, because it seemed like your hot little flight attendant recognized her well enough. But you're telling me she was lying about being your girlfriend?"

His knuckles turn white as he presses harder into the door, eyes blazing with anger. "I dated her once. But I cut things off with her months before she talked to you. She was jealous of you. She said anything she could to get you to leave."

My eyes well with tears, and I don't know if it's from anger, sadness, embarrassment, or maybe some combination of the three. "Can I go now?"

He hesitates a long time, watching me with eyes that don't look cold or disinterested. They look as possessive and hungry as the last time I saw him. I'm worried if I stand here too long I'll fall under his spell again, that I'll believe this mountain of a man really wants me--cares for me, even.

"For now," he says. "But if you think you're coming here was a coincidence, you're mistaken. We'll talk again, Kylie. Soon."

6

DAMIAN

After finding Kylie at the party last night, I still feel a rush of constant adrenaline, like I'm alive for the first time in three years. I found her. I finally fucking found her.

Every day I spent apart from her made me want her that much more until my need for her became an all-consuming obsession. Faleena stole three years I could've had with Kylie from me, and I'll never forgive her for that, but at least now I can start making up for lost time.

I've hired private investigators, done my own research, and I've even wasted hours wandering the airport where we first met, just hoping I'd have a chance to see her again and explain the truth to her, and for a chance to get her back. Fuck, I've practically had to become a stalker, but I don't regret any of it.

I got the lead last month when she took a job in San Francisco. I already owned a few pieces of property out here, so relocating was as simple as making a few phone calls to have my properties made ready. I've worked through acquaintances to invite her to at least five parties before this one, all of which were thrown just to get her to show up. Last night was the one that finally worked.

Maybe I could've just shown up at the office where she works, but I wanted a chance for her to remember why we were so right for each other. I wanted to bring her to one of my dungeons, where I could give her the kind of orgasms she deserves. But my little kitten is going to play hard to get, apparently.

I knew Kylie would probably be pissed at me, but I have to admit, I thought last night was going to end very differently. I hoped time would have cooled her anger and she could've heard reason, but it seems like while I've spent every day craving her more, she has been fueling the fans of misplaced anger.

It's not entirely bad, though. I have always enjoyed the hunt, and the idea of hunting for something I want as badly as her already has my cock hard. I haven't been with a woman since I had a taste of Kylie three years ago, and I'm so ready to have my hands on her and my cock buried deep in her tight pussy again that it's all I can do to wait.

So I don't.

THE PLACE she works is one of those depressing, glass boxes that house multiple businesses. I was planning to run by my office later, so I'm still wearing my suit, which draws attention as I step inside what appears to be a business casual kind of place. After a little asking around, I'm told the data entry center is on the third floor. The elevator opens up to a wide floor plan full of cubicles not quite high enough to hide the eyes of the men and women sitting at their computers, clacking away on keyboards with bored expressions.

One by one, pairs of eyes dart up to follow me as I move through the space, searching for Kylie. I don't make it far before a scrawny little man in a puke-yellow button-down stops me. He rakes a hand through his thinning hair and plants his hands on hips that are a little too prominent to belong to a man. "Can I help you?" he asks.

"Yeah. You could move so I don't have to pick you out of my shoes later."

His face pales a little, but to his credit he straightens his back, clearly used to being the top dog around this depressing place. "Right. I'm just going to have you stay right here while I call security."

"Do what you need to do," I say, pushing past him to continue my search.

"Hey!" He calls after me.

Everyone stops working now to watch with curious eyes over the tops of their cubicles.

A woman I don't recognize hops up and comes to stand beside me. She's a little taller than average with dirty blonde hair and a long, willowy neck. Pretty, but I can already see from the way she carries herself she's not my type. Hell, I haven't seen any woman was my type since I met Kylie. I guess my type *is* Kylie.

"Steve, look at him," she says, eying me appreciatively. "You can't just throw a man like this out to the curb."

"Amen," yells a woman from somewhere across the room, which is met with a few chuckles.

I ignore all of them, craning my neck to look through the cubicles. I see the back of a head, which catches my attention in the room full of people who are half-standing at their desks to stare my way.

"Kylie?" I ask.

The person with their back to me twitches. It's her. I'd recognize her dark, curly hair anywhere.

"Kylie," I say again more firmly. I have to push past the woman who confronted the manager and the little man who is trying to forcibly shove me back toward the exit now. I sweep my arm in front of me, knocking him aside so that he stumbles into a cubicle wall, eyes bulging with rage.

"If you don't--" he starts

"Back the fuck off," I growl, turning slowly to face him. "Go call security if you want, but if you come near me again I'll be happy to knock your tiny ass out."

Kylie is hastily shoving things into her handbag. She shoulders it and tries to hurry from her cubicle. I reach out, taking her by the arm.

Everyone still watches us, but I don't care. Just being near her again has my heart hammering. "Kylie," I say quietly.

She turns toward me with eyes red from crying.

"Who fucking hurt you?" I ask, lunging forward to cup her cheek and look her over. "Was it someone at the party? Give me a name."

"Stop," she says, voice shuddering. "Just stop." She pulls back, visibly gathering herself and squeezing her eyes shut. "Nobody hurt me. Nobody gets to hurt me anymore. You're the last one with that honor."

I clench my teeth so hard it hurts. I could fucking kill Faleena for this. If I had known Kylie was carrying around this much pain from what happened back on my private plane three years ago, I would have torn down every city in the fucking country until I found her and set this straight, I would've spent my fortune running ads and billboards telling her what a crock of shit Faleena fed her. "It shouldn't have taken me this long to find you," I say. "But I'm here now. Let me show you she was lying. Just give me a chance."

"It's not that easy."

"He's over here!" shouts Steve, who is guiding two security guards toward me from the elevators.

"We can make it that easy. Meet me. Give me one chance. Five minutes, even. That's all I ask. I'll be at Baker's coffee in an hour. It's just a block from here on the corner."

Her eyes well with tears, but she fights them back. The conflict is written so clearly on her face it tears at me like rusted knives. I can't stand that I put her through this. I shouldn't have ever let her from my sight back then and given Faleena a chance to fuck things up.

"Sir," says one of the security guards who reaches for my arm.

I pull my arm back, giving him a glare that clearly says he shouldn't touch me unless he wants to be dragged out of here unconscious. He gets the message and motions instead for me to head to the elevator.

"One hour," I say again to Kylie, who says nothing in return.

I'm escorted out of the building, drawing even more stares this time, but none of it registers. I can only think of the pain I saw in her face. Knowing I caused that makes me feel like the scum of the fucking Earth, and I know I'll never be able to make it up to her completely, but I'm sure as hell going to try.

I WAIT by myself in the coffee shop for two and a half hours before Kylie finally walks in. She looks self-conscious, and her vulnerability only makes me want her more. She spots me and walks over, slowly taking her seat but saying nothing.

"You have four minutes left," she says after a brief silence.

I raise my eyebrows. "I'd say four minutes thirty seconds, but--"

"Three minutes and fifty seconds," she says coldly.

Damn. "Ask me anything you want," I say. "I'll be a hundred percent honest."

"Was everything she told me a lie?"

"I don't know exactly what she told you, but Faleena was nothing to me. I met her at a club a few months prior to that day at the airport. We went on a handful of dates and I broke things off. No woman has ever held my interest for long, Kitten, except you. I've spent every day since we've been apart thinking of you, *looking* for you."

She shakes her head and looks out the window to our side. I

can practically see the emotions at war inside her. She's conflicted. Part of her probably wants to throw a coffee in my face and leave for good. The other part? I can only hope that part of her knows she feels something real between us, too, that all this talk isn't just crazy.

"Listen," I say, reaching across the table to grip her hand. She doesn't pull it back. "Some people think you need to go on a handful of dates to get to know someone. Me? I think that's bullshit. I knew you the moment I looked into your eyes. I knew you were a strong woman. I knew you were intelligent as hell, and I knew nobody--especially any men--had ever taken care of you the way you deserve. All I wanted was to be that man for you. It's still all I want."

She bites her lip and looks down at where our hands meet. "I want to believe you. That's why I'm so afraid to give you a chance," she says quietly. "I know it's probably not fair to take a stranger's word over yours, but then you're basically a stranger, too, aren't you?"

My eyebrows draw down. "You know that's not true. Look me in the fucking eyes and tell me I feel like a stranger to you."

She looks away, takes a deep breath, and sighs. I can see her coming to some kind of decision, one I hope involves a date with me. "If you knew the real truth about me you wouldn't be saying all this. No. No... I can't do this. You'll only run away when you get close and I'll be back where I started, except this time you'll break me."

Her lower lip quivers and she looks at her phone. "That's five minutes."

"Kylie," I say firmly, but she picks up her bag and rushes out of the shop.

I slam my fist on the table, making several nearby people jump and give me nervous glances. "The fuck are you looking at?" I ask at the college kid closest to me.

He picks up his bag and hurries outside, glancing over his shoulder before he leaves.

I lean back in my chair and run my hands across my face with a groan of irritation. *Fuck.* She is not making this easy. If I knew the whole truth? What was she talking about? What *truth* could there be that would make me want to run from her? There's nothing. I don't care if she has a dead body in her trunk. She's going to be mine, whether she believes it or not, and I'm just going to have to keep trying to convince her.

7

KYLIE

I lean my head against my apartment door and fight back tears for what seems like the twentieth time in two days. I'm not normally a crier, and I hate being such a mess right now, but I feel like I'm being pulled in a hundred different directions at once. Every atom in my body is screaming to reach out for Damian, to let him hold me and run his hands through my hair, to let him whisper those dirty thoughts of his in my ear and make my skin prickle with goosebumps. But I can't stop the small voice in the back of my head that keeps asking "what if?" What if Faleena was really telling the truth? Wouldn't a guy like the one she described to me lie and say whatever he thought would get him in my pants?

I think about little Dean and his sweet smile. I can't do that to him. I can't risk attaching myself to a guy who I'm not a hundred percent sure about. *Two hundred percent sure.* Even if he is my baby's father. I don't care how he makes my body feel or how good it would feel to simply be held again. I can't. And even if Damian was telling the truth? Even if it was all sincere and he really does want to try to make things work with me?

What's he going to think when he finds out I have a son. That *we* have a son.

"God," I groan, clutching my temples and sliding down to sit outside my apartment with my back to the door. Most guys would probably turn and run as soon as they find out I have a kid. And even if he didn't, what would he think if he found out I had *his* kid and didn't tell him about it for all these years? It doesn't even matter that I had no way to find him. Just the fact that I didn't try will be damning enough.

I hear little footsteps on the other side of the door and I'm suddenly falling backwards to bump into the ground, face toward the ceiling. Dean's little smiling face hovers over me. He belts out a giggle. "Mommy home!"

Angie, the nanny Alec paid for, comes from the kitchen with a crooked smile on her face. She's in her forties and has exactly the kind of stern, motherly attitude Dean needs in his life. If she wasn't way out of my budget, I'd snatch her up in a heartbeat to replace my normal sitter, but it's not an option. Dean's just going to be stuck with a pushover mom and a pushover babysitter once my time with Angie runs out.

"Sorry," she says. "He heard you coming up the stairs and wanted to surprise you."

"He succeeded," I say, grunting a little as I sit up and rub the back of my head.

Dean prods the back of my head when he sees me clutching it. "Oh no! Boo boo! Ice!" He screams before run-waddling to the fridge to get his little heart-shaped ice pack.

"Are you okay?" she asks, concern splitting her features when she sees my eyes, which I assume are red and puffy with mascara smeared underneath.

"I'm fine," I say. "It was just a rough day."

"I can stay till his bed time if you want to go in and take a nap."

Dean comes rushing back with the little red frozen heart held up like a trophy. "Ice!" He declares moments before tripping and falling flat on his face.

Angie and I both wince, hands going to our faces. Dean gets up, frowns down at his knees, as if trying to decide if this particular boo boo was tantrum worthy. "Oh no," he says happily. "Boo boo." With a self-satisfied smile, he plops down and presses the ice to his knee.

I grin at Angie, who smiles back. "He's a little trooper. I don't know if I've ever seen a tougher little guy."

"I wish I could say he got that from me," I say carelessly.

There's an awkward moment of silence. I don't talk about Dean's dad with anybody, and Angie has probably already picked up on that. Thankfully, someone knocks at the door, saving me from the discomfort.

I pull it open and see Damian, standing there in my hallway looking determined and so sexy it's not even fair. I squeeze out as quickly as I can, before Dean sees Damian or vice versa. That's *not* a conversation I want to have right now--or ever, for that matter.

"*What are you doing here?*" I hiss once the door's closed behind me.

"I'm not giving up on you. You said there was something that would make me run? Try me."

"Can we start with how you even know where I live?"

He flashes an unapologetic smirk. "Next time you try to run away from me, you might want to turn around every once in awhile to make sure I'm not following you."

"So you're pretty much stalking me?"

"If that's what it takes," he says.

I sigh, even though I want to be pissed or creeped out, I can't manage it. It's not fair to all the average looking guys of the world, but somehow being "stalked" by a guy like Damian feels flattering and exciting, no matter how I spin it. To think he's going to all this trouble just to get me to forgive him is going a long way toward making me want to give this thing a chance. I just hope I'm not being selfish and putting myself before Dean. If I knew I was doing this with his best interests at heart, I wouldn't be able to stop myself from practically begging Damian for a date. But my little guy on the other side of the door comes first. Before anything and everything.

Damian is obviously into some kind of crazy BDSM scene, if the place he took me to at the party is any indication. That, and the fact that he commands obedience like it's the most natural thing in the world, and he somehow makes submission feel so sweet. How could I knowingly bring a man like that into my son's life?

There's a thump at the door and the muffled sound of Dean's voice. "MeeeeOWWW," he yells playfully.

My eyes goes wide.

Damian squints past me. "Big cat..." he says.

I shift on my feet and tuck a hair behind my ear. "Yeah. I really need to put him on a diet."

"HeeeHAWWW," yells Dean.

I close my eyes in defeat. There's no way I'm convincing Damian I have a donkey in there, even if Dean's impression of a donkey *wasn't* terrible.

"Big cat and a little donkey..." says Damian slowly. He moves closer to me, eyes taking me in with a fiery intensity. "Invite me inside."

I've already seen how persistent Damian is. I know there's no use saying no to him now. If he knows I have a child, he'll never stop until he finds out the truth. My best hope is to let him see Dean, hope he doesn't see the resemblance, and then wait for him to decide he doesn't want to deal with the baggage like any other guy.

I open the door slowly.

Dean stands there in his cute little "Mommy's Best Man" shirt, which is tucked into his jean shorts. He looks up at

Damian with wide eyes, then notices the tattoos on Damian's arms.

"Oh no!" he says. "Dirty!" He runs toward the kitchen where we keep the wipes.

Damian looks to me with an amused glint in his eye. "I promise, I washed up before I came."

I give him a wry smile. "He has never seen tattoos."

"His dad doesn't have any?" asks Damian. His tone is light, but I can practically feel the weight behind the question.

"His dad isn't in the picture anymore."

Damian nods, relief clear in his features.

Dean comes waddling back with way too many wipes clutched in his small fist. "Sit!" he practically yells at Damian.

To my surprise, Damian sits down on the floor cross-legged. His sleeves are rolled halfway up his forearms, but he pulls them back above his biceps, giving me a mouth-watering view of tanned, tattooed skin pulled tight over perfectly formed muscle. Dean climbs into Damian's lap and frowns in consternation as he tries uselessly to wipe away the tattoos.

"Sorry, bud," says Damian with a grin. "I'm a dirty man. I don't know if any amount of wipes can fix that."

"Fix," repeats Dean, who still isn't giving up.

I lean in the doorway, watching the two of them together, trying with all my might not to get teary eyed and failing. I've never thought I'd see them together, and I didn't expect it to *look* so right. *God.* I didn't even realize they have the same smile, but I can see it so clearly now. Dean is so obviously Damian's son I'm surprised Damian didn't call me on it at his first glance.

"Go ask your mommy if you can have a marker," says Damian suddenly.

Dean pops up, dropping his wipes. He comes to stand below me, craning his neck to look up at me. "Markuh?" he asks.

"Fine," I say with a smile. "Go get one. *But be careful with it.*"

He hurries off to the drawer where we keep the arts and

crafts. I give Damian a long, curious look. "Do you have kids?" I ask.

"Hey, I think we're getting somewhere. She's asking me questions now."

I glare. "Do you?"

"No. But I've always wanted them."

"Well, you're really good with Dean," I say.

"Dean?" he asks. "It's a good name. Strong and a classic."

"Thanks," I say, blushing and feeling more relief than I should that he likes it.

Dean returns with a green washable marker. "Markuh," he declares, holding it up like the holy grail.

"See this?" asks Damian, who points to part of the tattoo on his arm. "This is a *tattoo*. Do you want one?"

"Yes," says Dean with an emphatic nod.

"Come here." Damian sits Dean on his knee and uncaps the marker. "Do you like cats?"

"MeeeOWW," says Dean.

Damian chuckles. "That's a yes if I've ever heard one. We're going to give you a cat tattoo on your arm."

"Arm," agrees Dean.

I realize Angie is standing in the doorway of the kitchen, watching with a happy little smile on her face. She shoots me a double thumbs up and makes some surprisingly suggestive gestures when Damian isn't looking.

I nearly snort out a laugh, but hold it in somehow. Watching the two of them together is going a long way toward changing my mind about how dangerous it would be to get involved with Damian. A *long* way. I've barely seen Dean interact with men before, and it's clear now how much he needs that kind of influence in his life. *We both do.*

"There. Meooow," says Damian.

"Cat!" yells Dean, who runs up to me and shows me. "Cat!"

"Oooh, it's so pretty, Dean." It actually is, too. "Are you an artist or something?" I ask Damian.

"Nah," he says. "I'm just really good at drawing cats."

I laugh. "Sure."

Damian stands up, brushing off his knees and rolling his sleeve back down. "Sorry," he says, noticing Angie. "I didn't even see you there."

"No, no. I was just on my way out. Dean begged me all day to take him to the park so I'm going to give Kylie a break," she says, winking at me and making one more gesture that I definitely wouldn't expect out of a woman I thought was prim and proper.

Dean claps his hands, hugs my leg, and to my surprise, he fist bumps Damian before following Angie out the door.

I cover my smile with my hand and nod to her as she goes.

"What would you have done if I didn't let you in?" I ask.

"Doesn't matter. Because I knew you were going to let me in."

As much as being around him again is filling me with butter-flies, it feels dangerous, like being with Damian is so all or nothing that there would be no turning back once I step over the ledge. Every guy before Damian felt like an open doorway--as easy to go in as it was to go out, but Damian? It's like he's a bottomless pit of lust and hunger and primal sexuality. There are no half-measures with him. The only way in is to plunge over the edge into his darkness, and once I've taken that step there will be no turning back, for better or worse.

I have to find a way to keep some kind of emotional distance so I don't get swallowed up in him. I just don't know how long I can keep it up.

"Jerk," I say.

He eyes glint with something dangerous. The look is gone as quickly as it comes though, replaced by a quick smile. "Do you draw the line at going on a date with a jerk? Because there's a party tonight and I was hoping I wouldn't have to show up alone."

"A date?" I ask. "Listen. I'm going to make this as clear as I can. I want what's best for my son. And yes, if there were no other factors involved, I'd love to go on a date with you. But I have to think of Dean. I can't risk bringing someone into our lives that I don't trust completely."

"Then let me prove you can trust me. Go on a date with me. No commitments. We'll go out as many times as you need to be convinced."

"I thought you said dates were pointless."

"When it comes to you, they are. *For me.* What matters is you. If you want to get to know me more, then that's what we'll do."

"What happened to Mr. Demanding?"

"There is a time and place for that," he says with a smile that makes my core tingle with heat. "We'll play by your rules. For now."

I swallow hard when my head fills with images of him standing over me while he reaches to undo his buttons, revealing that hard, muscular torso I've pictured so many times when the lights are off. He's been my guilty pleasure in the dark of night, and now that he's here for real, I can't fight it any longer. I have to give this a shot.

"I need to make sure Angie can watch Dean a little longer. And I have to read him a bedtime story before I go. It's our thing."

Damian throws his hands up in compliance. "Whatever you need, Kitten."

Kitten. That's what he called me all those years ago, and it's the first time he has used the pet name since he came back into my life. I can already feel his possessive grip tightening around me, and I hate how much I love it.

8

DAMIAN

"This is a really nice car," says Kylie. I can hear stiffness in her tone, like she's still not sure she made the right decision by coming with me.

"I always thought it would be different to be wealthy," I say, surprising myself by already letting my guard down and talking about my past. I never let women in, and even though I've devoted everything to finding Kylie again and making this happen, I still expected old habits to die hard. I guess not, though, because the words come freely, and they feel good coming out. "It's nothing like I thought it would be."

"How do you mean?" she asks. Maybe she can tell I'm giving her something I wouldn't even consider giving another woman because she leans in now, watching me with interested eyes as I drive us through the city.

"When you don't have money, it feels like it's the answer to all your problems. Sad? You think you'd be happier if you could just afford those things you want. Lonely? If you had money, you would have people knocking down your door. Unfulfilled? With money, you could literally do anything you want. The truth I've found is once you have money, you're forced to take the first real look at yourself you've ever taken. You strip away the excuses and the what ifs. You can't hang your motivation on what it would be like to make it big anymore. You have to look in the mirror and ask yourself if you're happy every morning, and if you're not? There's nothing left stopping you from going after what you want."

"Did you go after it? The thing you wanted."

"Discovering what I wanted took many years. But once I knew? Yes. I never stopped. I thought about it every hour of every day. I poured all my energy into it until I made it happen."

"What was it?" she asks.

"You," I say.

She looks at her lap, cheeks flashing so red I can see it even in the dim light. "You say the right things," she says quietly. "And I want to believe them. I really do."

"You don't need to explain it," I say. "You're being careful. Doing what's best for Dean. I admire that."

Kylie's sitter agreed to watch Dean as late as she needed, which is good, because there's no telling how late I'm going to keep her out tonight. Like most nights, there are a handful of BDSM clubs we could visit, including an exclusive party I agreed to have at my mansion, but the party will go on whether I'm there or not. Tonight isn't about me, though. It's about trust. Kylie needs to know she can trust me before we can move forward in any meaningful way, so I'm not going to confuse things by bringing her to a club--not just yet, at least.

I may be practically ready to burst at the seams from my need to take her again in all the ways I've had three years to imagine, but I have larger goals than my own carnal pleasures. Ever since I saw her in the airport and felt that spark of connection ignite between us, I've wanted one thing more than anything else: her happiness. I'm sure I've said as much to women in the past, but it was nothing but lip service--a flattering phrase to draw out a smile or make them feel cared for.

Kylie is different. She always has been. There's a perfect innocence to her. Not the kind of innocence men often talk or care
about. I don't give a shit if she's been with men before me or if she
has sinned. Her purity is deeper than any of that. I know there's a
piece of herself she holds close to her chest. She guards it so carefully that I doubt even she even realizes she's doing it anymore,
but Kylie is damaged. Whether she suffered something traumatic
or was just beat down by the day-to-day of her life, I may never
know, but I know it made her put up walls, walls that even she
can't get through.

More than anything, I want to bring those walls down, not
just for my own satisfaction, but for hers. I want her to be free,
and I know I'm the man to release her. I just need to convince her.

"I want to take you somewhere special, but the dress code is...
complicated," I say. "We need to go on a quick shopping run
before dinner so you have the appropriate attire."

"I don't know if I can--"

"Everything is on me, Kitten. All I want you to do tonight is
relax. Everything is taken care of. Everything will be perfect."

WE ARRIVE at the restaurant a little over an hour later. Kylie is
wearing the dress I bought her--a simple black thing that fits her
so unbelievably well I am seconds from throwing away my good
intentions of keeping her out of the clubs, and my bed, tonight.
My cock is also throbbing because I picked out the swimsuit she
wears beneath the dress as well, and the similarities to our time
in the airport three years ago are not lost on me. Not at all.

"I still don't see why I couldn't just change into a swimsuit
when it was time," she says, although she doesn't say it in a
whining kind of way. I'm happy to hear a hint of teasing in
her voice.

She knows damn well why I insisted she wear the swimsuit
beneath her dress. She just wants to hear it out loud. "Because the last

time I fucked a woman, I was surprised to find she was wearing a bikini beneath her dress instead of panties."

"The last time you..." she starts, eyes widening a little with surprise.

"Yes, Kitten," I say as we approach the front of the restaurant, which is a modern building with sleek blue lights that backs up to the ocean. "I waited for you. And if you decide you aren't ready, I'll keep waiting as long as I have to."

She tucks a lock of hair behind her ear and smiles. "Somehow, I doubt that."

"You'll learn to trust me before long." *And then you'll learn to submit.* Fucking hell, it's hard to walk comfortably when Kylie has me hard all the time, but I know once I've built the proper foundation of trust, there is never going to be anything as sweet as breaking her in as my submissive. She'll learn to relish it as well, in giving herself up to me and testing the strength of the trust and the bond we'll form, knowing it's stronger every time it stands up to the test.

"At least one of us is confident of that," she says, but her voice carries the same note of teasing.

It's good to hear her loosening up, even if it's just a little.

The maitre d' welcomes us at the door. "Mr. Price," he says with raised eyebrows. "It's an honor to have you and your lovely guest tonight. We'll prepare a table and equipment for you at once. Please, feel free to enter the diving room at your earliest convenience. We'll clear the queue."

I nod my thanks, walking Kylie through the restaurant with my hand splayed wide on her back and my body language clearly saying she's mine to anyone who might try to enjoy too long a look at her.

"You really weren't kidding about the diving thing?" she asks nervously.

"You'll be fine. It's just with snorkels. Although I guess the harpoon gun could be a little intimidating."

She pales a little. "Harpoon gun?"

"How did you think we'd catch dinner? With a fork and knife?"

She glares at me and I can't help smirking. There will come a time when she'll learn a look like that is going to earn her a special kind of punishment, one that leaves both of us sweating and breathless, but not yet. There will be plenty of time for all that.

We pass a small group of well dressed men and women who chatter in the lobby outside the dive room while they snack of hors d'oeuvres. Kylie draws jealous eyes from the women and hungry eyes from the men, but I pay it no mind. The whole world could be condemning us for all I care, so long as she's mine, nothing else matters.

There are several dressing rooms inside the dive room, and I excuse myself to slip into compression shorts and set my suit and tie aside. Kylie goes into her own dressing room and changes out of her dress. I take my time enjoying the view when she emerges. Her swimsuit is a black one-piece with several strategically placed cutouts, which give more than enough room for my imagination to fill in the blanks.

She holds her arms in front of her body when she comes out, clearly self-conscious, but I love how she can't keep her eyes from wandering my bare torso greedily.

I give a sharp look to the dive instructor, who catches my meaning immediately. *Don't even dare look at her.* He carefully keeps his eyes fixed somewhere between a few feet over my head and the floor while he explains how the equipment works and the general safety guidelines.

Basically, you point the harpoon gun at a fish, pull the trigger, and don't forget to go up for air when you feel like you need to breathe. Nothing complicated.

"Come here," I say to Kylie. I lead her to the snorkels and masks, which look like they were just cleaned. I help her get hers on before securing my own. I hand her a harpoon gun next, jumping a little when she swings it in front of me. I laugh, reaching to take her hand and point it at the ground. "Careful with that. I don't think they'll cook me, even if you stick me with a harpoon."

"Sorry," she says with a laugh. "I'm a little nervous."

"Don't be. I'll be right beside you the whole time. You'll be fine."

We walk to the edge of the wood platform, which ends in a six inch drop straight into the open ocean behind the restaurant. The water is lit by dozens of floodlights placed by the restaurant in the fishing grounds, so I can see quite a ways down despite the time of night. I take Kylie's hand and give her a tug as I jump in, taking her with me. She yelps just before we hit the water.

We sink down in a cascade of bubbles. Kylie spins slowly around, taking in the scene around us. The floodlights are carefully placed to avoid making the underwater ecosystem look artificial. The light filters through cracks in the coral and between large rocks, giving everything a greenish blue glow. Fish are everywhere, some swimming in schools of a hundred and no larger than my thumb nail, while other, larger fish drift by, some close enough to be illuminated by the lights and others nothing more than shadows in the distance.

Kylie motions to me that she's going up for air.

I follow her to the surface, which is still inside the room we jumped down in. "What if there are sharks?" she asks.

I hold up my harpoon gun. "I'll keep you safe, Kitten. Just worry about finding a fish that looks good enough to eat."

She gives me a somewhat skeptical look, but takes a deep breath and dives back down. I follow after her, letting her get just enough ahead of me that I can enjoy the view of her ass while she kicks her way through the water. I'm hard as a rock in seconds from the thought of having her again. The darker part of me is trying to figure out if I could make her cum before we had to go up for air, but I told myself I'd give her time. I know there's a sexual attraction between us. That much is abundantly clear. What I don't know is if Kylie feels like she can trust me enough to let me into her life. *And her son's life.* So I'm keeping focused on what matters most tonight. I don't just want to fuck her one last time. I want to make her mine for the rest of my life.

She pulls her harpoon gun up and squeezes the trigger. There's a small burst of bubbles and the harpoon bursts out, missing a fish by about ten feet. I laugh, releasing a burst of bubbles that draws her glare. She makes a gesture that seems to say, *and you can do better?*

I take aim and fire, but my shot misses almost as badly as hers. I curse in annoyance, but my irritation is forgotten when I see the delighted smile on Kylie's face. She gives me a taunting waggle of her eyebrows from behind her goggles. She presses the button to retract her harpoon, which is connected to the gun by a string. She aims at the same fish and fires again, this time catching it with a direct hit. She does an adorable celebratory dance underwater that looks like something between drowning and a seizure before kicking up to the surface.

I follow her back up and take a deep, refreshing breath of air once we're on the surface again. "Nice shot," I say.

Her wide smile falters. "I feel kinda bad. I just shot him..."

I can't help laughing. "Him? You mean the fish?"

"Yes, the fish. He's just..." she pulls in the line from her gun and hoists the fish above water. His fin is still flapping slowly. "Oh my God. He's in pain," she says, horrified.

"Here. Close your eyes," I say.

"What are you going to do?"

"Don't you trust me?" I ask.

She watches me for a few seconds before closing her eyes with the faintest hint of a smirk.

I detach the harpoon from my gun and sever the fish's spine as humanely as I can. "It's done," I say. "He won't suffer anymore."

She blows out a breath, head bobbing a little as she kicks to stay afloat. "I know it's dumb. I eat fish and meat all the time. It's just different to kill it myself."

"It's not dumb. It's kind. *You're* kind."

She looks away. "Well, you still need to catch a fish for yourself. And with that aim of yours, we should probably get to it before they all go to sleep."

I give her a mock glare. "I only missed so you wouldn't feel as bad about missing like you did."

"Right," she says, biting her lip. "Then it'll be no problem for you to hit the next one."

"No problem," I say.

It's nearly half an hour later when I finally manage to harpoon a fish. We're both exhausted from swimming, and I don't know about Kylie, but my stomach is already rumbling. "Come on," I say. "This way."

"Shouldn't we be swimming back toward the dock?" she asks.

"I planned a little surprise for us."

"Should I be afraid?"

"Probably. I'm about as good at driving a boat as I am at shooting fish with harpoons."

I take her to a section of the restaurant's dock where a small boat is tied up. I help Kylie inside first and then climb in myself. We both sigh with relief to be out of the water and take a moment to enjoy sitting. I set our catches on the side of the boat and turn on the engine, which is little more than an outboard motor with a handle for steering at the back of the boat.

"Where are we going?" she asks.

"It wouldn't be much of a surprise if I told you."

We're both knocked to the side when I steer the boat into a wave at the wrong angle because my eyes were focused on Kylie's cleavage and the way the drops of water from her hair are trailing a path that I wouldn't mind joining them on down between her breasts.

"You weren't kidding about being a bad driver," she says.

"I was afraid of water most of my life," I say. "I guess I'm behind the curve on nautical pursuits because of it."

"You were afraid of water?" she asks, frowning. "I don't take you for the type to frighten easily."

"I had an older brother who was trying to walk across a waterfall when I was fourteen. His name was Kyle. I spent my life looking up to him. He was invincible, as far as I was concerned. It was a stupid thing he had done hundreds of times with his friends, but he stepped on a slick rock, lost his balance, and hit his head before he fell about twenty feet down. By the time they found him at the bottom of the river, he had already drowned. After that... it felt like I was drowning if I even thought about getting in water above my knees." I laugh at myself, surprised again by how much I seem to be telling Kylie without planning to. "Listen to me, talking like I'm on some fucking therapist's couch."

"No," she says, reaching to touch my knee. "If I am going to trust you, I need to *know* you. What happened between us three years ago was..." she clears her throat and gives up searching for the right words. "What I'm trying to say is, yes, I felt something. I felt like I wanted to be part of your life, as crazy as that was. But I can't afford to attach myself to a mystery anymore. It's like I told you, I have Dean to think about. Maybe before him I could've just enjoyed the ride and waited to see where it took me. But if this is going to work now, I need to know you. The real you. So don't apologize for it."

I nod my head. "It's just not me. Talking about myself like this. I'm used to keeping everyone at arm's length--hell, I'm used to keeping them outside the fucking door."

9

KYLIE

He pulls the boat up to a sandy patch of land that juts out from the beach, where a small team of two chefs and a waiter are standing beside a smoking grill. There's even a table set up with candles.

"This is for us?" I ask.

"Just for us," he says before hopping out of the boat and offering me his hand.

"Don't take this the wrong way, because I'm extremely grateful either way, but why did you bother having me pick out a dress if we were going to eat out here?"

"I wasn't about to have you walk into the restaurant looking this fucking sexy. Whether you're ready to trust me or not, I'm sure as hell not ready to let other men see you like this."

I notice both of the chefs and the server are female and smile a little despite myself. I don't know if I've ever met a man more possessive than Damian, and I can't say the idea of being wanted so badly and so greedily by him doesn't make my skin prickle with excitement. Somehow he manages to make nothing but the black compression shorts he wears look classy and mouth-wateringly sexy at the same time.

Even wet, his hair seems to fall perfectly over his piercing blue eyes. The small beads of water that occasionally run down his muscled frame catch my eyes, dragging them down his carved chest and rack of perfectly defined abs, and down more to the bulge I would think was too big to be his cock if I hadn't experienced it first-hand already. In some ways I thought I had managed to embellish it in my memory, but I can see the outline clearly now, and I know I was remembering it just right.

I press my thighs together against the growing heat I feel between my legs. *I'm sorry, Dean. I'm doing my best to handle this the right way. I really am.*

The guilt rises up like something black and vile, tainting all the excitement and happiness I feel. It's not the first time tonight, either. Every time I start to let go and enjoy myself, I'm haunted by the idea that I'm being careless. Worse, that I'm doing something that will put my son in danger.

And yet nothing about Damian is making me feel like I'm in danger. His idea of sex is vastly different than anything I ever imagined, and he practically radiates sexuality, but that doesn't *have* to mean he's a bad person. I need to give him a chance. It could turn out that he's wrong for me and Dean, and if that's true, I can walk away. But if I never give him a real chance, and in doing so give *myself* a chance to be happy then how will I know? I won't be able to go back and change it if I push him away now.

I force the guilt back down, wishing it would stay there because I have nothing to feel guilty about. I'm a responsible adult and I am allowed to date.

"This is beautiful," I say, but I forget to remove my eyes from the outline of his cock against his pants, where I was absent-mindedly staring while wrapped in thought.

"You can take a closer look if you want, but I may need to send the staff away."

Blood rushes to my cheeks. "The table. This. It's very sweet and thoughtful of you to set this up."

"Don't give me too much credit. I was honestly trying to figure out a way to keep your clothes off as long as I could. This was the best idea I had."

I laugh as he guides me into a chair at the table and lets his hand graze my ass. The quick touch makes my pulse race and fills my thoughts with dirty and dark desires. He takes his seat across from me with a knowing look on his face.

"Well, whether your intentions were good or not, this has been great. I've never been on a date like this before. Just movies and chain restaurants, pretty much. Maybe mini golf here and there."

"So it is a date?" he asks.

I sigh. "I forgot I was trying to keep you hanging on that."

The chefs take the fish we caught and begin filleting them right by the water on a cutting board. I half-watch, but I can barely draw my attention away from the way the candle light flickers in Damian's eyes as he watches me. His attention doesn't waver, not even for a second. He's *consumed* by me, and I've never felt so flattered by a man's attention.

Before long I'm just as entranced, unable to look away in what must be several minutes of wordless communication like nothing I've ever experienced. I'd normally find my eyes darting away from a man's after a few seconds of silence, overcome by awkwardness and the impulsive need to fill the silence. But with Damian?

I feel comfortable. I listen to the water lapping at the sand to our side, to the crackle of wood burning beneath the grill, and to the rustle of wind through the palm trees beside us. The smell of freshly cooked fish begins to fill the air as well, mingling with the sweet salty smell of the ocean.

"You're beautiful," he says.

"Took you a while to think of that one."

He smirks. "I didn't see you complaining."

The server, a smallish woman with blonde hair tied back in a severe ponytail brings us plates. "We have two fresh lobster cakes crusted with panko. The sauce is a jalapeño lemon drizzle. Please enjoy."

I give Damian an *ooh so fancy* wiggle of my eyebrows. He half-smiles.

"I think I've only ever had crab cakes. And those were imitation crab," I say.

"You'll enjoy these, then."

I pick up my fork, looking at the food and not feeling as sure as he does that I'll enjoy it. I've never been a fan of spicy foods, and the idea of lemon and jalapeños mixed together sounds kind of unappealing. Still, I don't want to be rude. I'm sure this whole night cost a fortune, including the food, and I'm not about to be ungrateful by turning my nose up.

I take a forkful and bite in. The crust on the lobster cake is perfectly crisp in a way that complements the smooth, creamy interior. The first taste that hits my tongue is a savory blend of herbs in the breadcrumbs. The rich lobster flavor comes through next, followed by a sweet bite of spice from the jalapeño and then the acidic bite of the lemon is quick on its heels to neutralize the burn on my tongue.

"Oh my God," I say. "That's so good."

"I know. I come here all the time, and these are a big part of the reason."

"Do you bring a lot of women here?" I ask. I mentally scold myself as soon as the words are out. *Really? Could you have possibly fabricated a sentence to sound more needy and jealous than that? Of course he brings other women here, he--*

"It would probably sound less sad to say I do," he says, sounding unfazed by my immature question. "In all honesty I haven't even looked at another woman that way since I laid eyes on you. I always thought men who talked like that in absolutes with women were full of shit. They'd say once they met their wife, they stopped noticing other women. I never believed it until you."

I swallow hard, not failing to notice the way he might have just implied he could see me as a wife. He really doesn't move slowly, does he?

"Say I decide I can really trust you completely to be part of my life and my son's life... Have you thought about the possibility that I might not be everything you've spent three years imagining I am? What if you couldn't stand living with me, or the way I sing in the car? As much as it's nice to hear all the things you're saying, I don't know how you can *know* with so much certainty."

He sets his fork down, leaning forward just enough to intensify the effect his eyes have on me. No matter how much he looks at me, I can't stop wanting more of his attention. Having those eyes of his on me feels like a drug, one I can't get enough of.

"I know people," he says. "It's how I made my fortune. It's part of the work I do every day. It has always been a gift of mine. Everyone says so much more than they realize through their body language, and I've been fluent in that language as long as I can remember. You're not saying it, but what you're really worried about is that my sexual needs will be more than you can handle."

A jolt of surprise runs through me. Whether I realized it or not, I think he's right. That fear was at the heart of what I was saying. "And what if it is more than I can handle?" *Is it a deal breaker?* That's the real question I'm asking, and maybe the most important. It might even be the only thing standing between us. What if I can't dive into the lifestyle he wants. What if I can't live my life as some kind of submissive to him?

"I'll make this as clear as I can," he says. "My sexual appetite revolves around you. You know what gets me off? You know the only fucking thing that has brought me any kind of pleasure for the last three years? The idea of making you cum."

One of the chefs pauses, knife held in her hand. I feel a flush of embarrassment when I realize they can probably hear every word he's saying right now, but judging from the looks they are exchanging, they are all wishing they were sitting where I am right now.

"I don't care if you cum because I'm fucking you missionary while you wear a bathrobe with the lights off, because we're sneaking a quick fuck in a place where people could find us, or because I've got your hands tied up over your head and I'm spanking your ass with a paddle. All I care about is giving you the hardest, most life-shattering orgasms I can. *That* is my sexual appetite."

I feel a little dizzy, and my pussy is so hot and wet it feels like I need to jump back in the ocean or...

No. The "or" isn't an option. Not yet. Damian knows what to say to make me want to leave logic and good sense at the door, but I still don't know enough about him.

"That's--well," I say, clearing my throat and taking a drink from the glass of wine I just noticed by my plate. "That's good to know."

I shift in my chair at the office, struggling to think of anything but him. I let out a long breath, shaking my head.

"So?" asks Melina, who rolls her chair over during Greg's usual bathroom break.

"So what?" I ask, but we both know exactly what she's talking about.

She gives me a dry look. "Don't make me beg for details. You know I'll do it. I'll get down on my knees. I'll suck your toes."

"Ew," I laugh. "I'll tell you as long as you promise *not* to suck my toes."

"Deal. Why, were they already sucked last night on your wild date with Mr. Billionaire?"

"No, for starters. And what makes you think he's a billionaire?"

Melina clicks her tongue in disappointment. "Young Kylie. One of these days I'll introduce you to this crazy thing called the internet, where all the answers you could ever want are right there at your fingertips."

"I'm not an idiot. I just," I clear my throat, realizing I'm about to admit just how reckless I've been so far. "I don't actually know his last name."

"I didn't either," she says. "I didn't even know his first name. But there are only so many billionaires in the world, so finding a list of billionaires with homes in California wasn't hard at all. Then I just had to cross-reference the names with pictures *annnd*, tada! In less than four minutes I had a sizzling picture of Mr. Damian Price on my computer screen. Thirtieth richest man in the US, business and real estate tycoon, blah blah blah. Point is, he has a lot of money, and he's hot as hell. *And you went on a date with him last night.* So you had better spill every last detail or so help me God, I'll take you into the broom closet and waterboard you."

"You'll waterboard me? First you want to suck my toes and now you're going after my boobs?"

She spits out a surprised laugh. "*Waterboard,* Kylie. You're thinking of motor-boating. Waterboarding is torture, motor-boating is... never mind. The point is I'll torture your innocent little ass if I have to."

I grin. "You're absolutely crazy."

"Yeah," she says, bulging her eyes threateningly. "So don't test me, bitch."

I laugh, covering my mouth quickly incase Greg has lurked back into the office. The sound of laughter draws his attention as quickly as blood in the water draws a shark. He can smell fun from miles off and will come to stomp it out as fast as he can.

I spend the next few minutes filling her in on every detail of the date. When I'm finished, her eyes are dreamy. She leans back and raises her eyebrows with a satisfied sigh. "Wow. I didn't even know they had a place like that. And the whole private dinner on the beach thing? That was a nice touch. Very nice. So what next? Are you seeing him tonight? This afternoon? On your lunch break? I need more!"

"Calm down, I mean, I don't even know for sure. He said he wanted to see me again, but we didn't set anything in stone."

"He drove you back home, you didn't even kiss him, and he just said he wanted to see you again?"

I shrug, hoping she doesn't see the guilty look on my face. I may not have told her absolutely everything, like the fact that Damian walked me to my door and gave me a kiss that still has my knees feeling like warm butter.

I kissed him even though I told myself to wait. But I don't know who could've resisted in my position. Who could stay cold under those blazing blue eyes of his?

"He might have been a little more specific than that," I admit.

"Like how?"

"He said he wanted to bring me to a BDSM club. He said I didn't have to *do* anything, but he wanted me to see what it was like to be his submissive for a night."

Melina's jaw literally drops. "He's into BDSM? Are you serious?"

"You're surprised? I met him at that crazy party you made me go to. You know, the one with the room full of people in red clothes who were slapping each other with whips and having sex out in the open?"

"I already told you I didn't know about that little section of the party. I totally would've crashed that area if I knew."

"Well, do you remember the guy I told you about three years ago in the airport? The computer cords he tied around my wrists..."

She claps her hands to her face. "It's *him?*" she gasps. "Shut up!"

"No!" I hiss, looking around for Greg. "*You* shut up before you bring Greg down on us both."

She rubs her hands over her knees, shaking her head. "This is so insanely cool, Kylie. You know you have to go right? You need to fuck him. Not just for yourself. Not just for me. For every woman alive. You need to go to that club and be his little submissive, whatever that even means, and you need to enjoy every fucking second of it. Do you understand me? I swear on my mother's grave, I'll disown you if you pass this up."

I roll my eyes, smiling a little. "You can't swear on your mother's grave if she's not dead yet."

"Just because she's still alive doesn't mean we haven't ordered the headstone."

"Seriously?" I ask, frowning in disgust.

She tries to look offended, but can't pull it off. "It doesn't matter if we've ordered the stupid headstone. All that matters is you and him going to that club. I'll watch Dean for you if I have to."

"Angie's still with me for another couple days, thanks to Alec."

"See? You have no excuse. Literally no excuse."

I rub my temples. "You are like a bulldog sometimes. You know that? You just grab on and don't let go until you get what you want."

She snaps her teeth playfully at me.

I laugh. "I'll go, but only so you'll get off my back about it."

DAMIAN HELPS me out of his car in front of a place in a very ritzy part of the city that looks like a nondescript brick box. "This is it?" I ask, feeling a little unimpressed. I was expecting a sleek, modern style building with big floodlights or something. Maybe a huge neon sign of a woman with a whip.

"High profile clients," he says. "They would rather not broadcast what kind of club this is to anybody who happens to be driving by. You'll find senators, actors, TV personalities, doctors, and any other type of person you can imagine inside. I'm not just talking about the men, either."

I take in a deep breath, feeling my stomach flutter with nerves. Damian brought me something to wear, and I'm already feeling self-conscious in it even though there is hardly anybody nearby to see me. The dress fits loosely, but the material is thin enough I could see my underwear and the outline of my body with relative ease. When I tried telling him there was no way I could go out in public like this, he assured me I'd feel even more out of place if I went in there dressed conservatively.

I'm just glad Dean was already asleep when I left. I could never let him see me in something like this, even if he's still too young to understand. As much as all of this is exciting me, the sneaking around after Dean goes to bed has me reexamining everything. Isn't that exactly the kind of thing I was afraid Damian would bring? I don't want to feel like I have to hide my life from my son. Yes, it may be my sex life, but should my sex life really be such a big part of my life that I have to go out of the way to hide it from him?

"There are a few rules once we go inside," he says, turning to face me. He looks mouth-watering, as usual. His suit is black--fitting him snug in the right places so that it emphasizes his masculine frame perfectly. He wears a white collared shirt beneath and a black tie, making the simple colors somehow look striking. Even with a body like his, it's his eyes that always demand my attention. They carry so much weight it's like they have a gravity of their own, drawing my eyes up and up until I'm locked into those blazing blue eyes that always seem to be full of heat.

"Rules?" I ask. "Like the club's rules?"

"Some of them. Some of them are my rules for you," he says with a very serious tone and expression that makes me gulp down my response. "The club rules are based on what type of jewelry you wear. The more jewelry, the more off-limits you are. A necklace means you have a dom," he says, pulling a necklace from his jacket pocket and putting it around my neck."

I grin a little, feeling my cheeks burn. *I have a dom. I'm his.* But my dom doesn't know we have a son together. The thought sends a guilty stab of panic through me. Somewhere along the way it started to feel like he deserved to know. Hell, he always deserved to know, but I was being overly cautious. I knew if he knew the full truth about Dean, he'd stop at nothing to be part of his life. And if I didn't want to be part of Damian's life, there's no question about whether he has the financial means to take Dean from me. Not that I think he'd do that, it's just... Now that I'm getting to know him more, I know I should've told him the moment he first saw him. I should tell him now.

Except now I'm afraid of what might happen. What if he walks away? What if withholding the truth makes him so angry with me that he doesn't want to be with me anymore? Worse, what if he decides to take Dean from me? Using an expensive army of lawyers to teach me a lesson?

He wouldn't do that. I'm only thinking those kinds of things because they make it easier for me to avoid doing what I need to do. I'll tell him. Tonight. I don't know *when,* but I'll tell him.

"Bracelets mean your dom isn't willing to share. One bracelet," he says, sliding a diamond studded bracelet onto my wrist, "means your dom doesn't want another man to touch you. Two," he says, sliding on another. "Means your dom doesn't want another man to speak to you. And three," he says with no hint of a smile, "means your dom doesn't want any men to make eye contact with you."

I look up at him seriously. "What if I accidentally look at someone?"

He grips my chin, tilting my eyes up to his. "Then I'll have to punish you."

A chill runs through me, but it's not entirely cold. This is

another side of him. I've seen him with his guard down. I've seen
that he can be sweet, considerate, and thoughtful. He's good with
Dean, too. But this side of him? It reminds me of what he was like
in that conference room. And I'd be lying if I said I didn't like it.
The truth is I still feel the same thrill and freedom from being
commanded, from being *dominated.*

He takes out a pair of diamond earrings and puts them in
my ears.

"What do these mean?" I ask, wondering what other possible
restrictions there could be.

"They mean your dom bought you earrings and wanted to see
you in them."

I laugh.

He watches me approvingly. He doesn't smile, but there's a
slight change in his eyes that shows his amusement. I brace
myself for tonight. Yesterday, I enjoyed the lighter side of
Damian, he was almost playful. I could see myself falling head
over heels for *that* Damian. At the same time, this serious, almost
scary side of him is incredibly sexy. I don't know if the effect he
has on me will fade with time, but right now, I know I'm helpless
when he's this way.

It's the same sense of power that made me do something so
crazy I never would've even dreamed it three years ago, and I can
already feel that I'm at his mercy as completely as I was that day.

"Now for my rules," he says.

*More rules? What more could there be? Don't look at, talk to, or
touch any other guy in this place. What other trouble could I possibly
get into?*

"Inside, you'll call me Sir. You'll stay within arm's reach of me
at all times. You will treat my word like law. If I say it, you will do
it. And the most important rule is to use the safe words. Yellow
means you're nearing your limit, and red means stop."

"You won't be angry with me?" I ask.

"Kitten," he says, stroking my cheek with his thumb and

pulling me to him. "My only goal is your pleasure. My job as your dom is to challenge you, to bring you to your limit, to find thrills you never would on your own, and to give you the most mind-shatteringly perfect orgasms you've ever had. A relationship between a dom and his submissive requires more trust than a normal relationship. Much more. If I'm going to bring you to the edge of your comfort, I need to trust that you'll tell me if it goes too far. And you need to trust that I won't be angry if you stop me. Is that clear?"

"Yes."

"Yes, Sir," he corrects. "The next one will cost you."

"Cost me what?" I ask.

"You'll be punished, and my punishments can get creative."

"But I'm supposed to enjoy the punishment, right? What if I just disobeyed you because I *wanted* to be punished?"

He shows me the first sign of his more relaxed self and grins. "Then I'd find ways to make sure my kitten didn't behave so mischievously. The relationship between dominants and submissives isn't just about sex. Honestly, the sex is secondary. The true reward is the bond. There's no stronger bond on earth than the bond we could form if we put our trust in each other completely."

I nearly tell him about Dean right then, but listening to him talk about the club already has me itching to go inside. I want what he's promising. I want it so badly it hurts. If my biggest worry about him is that I can't trust him to be in our son's life, then what better way to learn if I can trust him than this? I'm ashamed to admit it, but I'm also so turned on right now I don't think I could make myself get the words out. I want him too badly. I want to be his again, even if it's just one last time.

"I want to try," I say.

He bends his neck to kiss me softly on the lips.

I lean into it, savoring the taste and the way his powerful arms encircle me, making me feel small and safe at the same time. He pulls back with what I think is more than a hint of reluctance. For a second, it looks like he might push me back into the car and take me there, but he must overcome the desire, because he puts his hand on my lower back instead.

"This way, Kitten."

The two men standing outside the door who look more like secret service than bouncers nod to him and open the door.

The club interior appears to be lit entirely by candlelight and it's like nothing I've ever seen. We walk directly into what seems to be a main gathering area that branches off into several smaller sections and hallways. The walls are paneled in deep, rich woods and lined with alcoves that hold candles. Chandeliers holding dozens of lit candles hang beautifully from the ceiling as well. I scan the crowd, which is bigger than I thought it would be, but I'm careful not to make eye-contact with any of the men.

Many wear masks, not unlike what I saw at the masquerade party I went to with Melina and Alec, but some don't. The men all wear expensive suits, though none make theirs look nearly as good as Damian does, I notice with pride. Damian was right about my clothes. Compared to what many of the women are wearing, I still look prudish even with a see-through dress.

One woman wears a leather bikini, the top has open holes for her nipples, which are pierced with three silver rods. Another wears a dress even more transparent than mine but she's completely naked beneath. Her dom has a silver leash around her neck and he's leading her to one of the darkened rooms in the back.

"Am I allowed to make any rules?" I ask. "Like that you don't get to look at any of these women?"

Damian looks down to me, taking my hands and making me face him. "There's only one woman I want to look at. The one I spent the last three years of my life searching for, and the one I will do anything to keep from slipping away again. *They are nothing,* Kitten."

I bite my lip. I want to believe him. I really do, but my self-doubt nags at me, asking why a man like him would possibly choose to look at me when there are so many beautiful half-naked women around. I've done my best to keep in shape after having Dean, but my hips are definitely more full than they were before, and I even have a few stretch marks now that I'm sure none of these women have. "So if I can't look at the men and you don't look at the women, why do we come here?"

"To show you off, for one," he says. "Every man here would kill for a chance with you, but they won't get it. You're mine, and I want everyone to know it. There are also some unique experiences we can find here that would be difficult to find elsewhere."

I try and fail not to smile stupidly at the thought of being shown off. I've never thought of myself as the kind of woman a man would show off. I probably would've thought the idea was insulting if anyone else had suggested it, but like everything else with Damian, it feels different coming from him.

"Come," he says. "I'll show you."

I follow him to a room lit by blue flames, which cast the two dozen or so people inside in a transfixing, icy glow. It's only once we're inside that I see what's happening on stage. I instinctively take a step back, like I've just walked in on something private that I shouldn't be seeing, but Damian's reassuring hand on my back and the other people watching, tell me I'm not intruding.

A woman on stage is lying face down on something that looks a little bit like a massage table, if it had been modified by a middle-age torturer. Her legs are splayed out, held by what look to be adjustable leg cushions and straps. Her arms are free, but another leather strap holds her down by the shoulders. A man with a black hood over his face from the nose up is kneeling between her legs, eating her out. Two more men stand on either side of her, completely naked except for black masks. She grips their cocks in her hands and masturbates them as her head slowly rolls from side to side with her moans.

The jealous part of me is relieved that Damian can't really see much of her naked body.

"Back here," says Damian, who leads me to the corner of the room, where I can still see what is happening on stage but we're out of the immediate view of spectators. "You like to watch, don't you? I saw the way your eyes were drawn to the stage."

I open my mouth to speak but snap it closed again, unable to decide what I should say.

He shakes his head. "No, Kitten. You're trying to figure out what I want to hear. Remember, there's one thing and one thing alone I care about here. Your pleasure. If my Kitten likes to watch, she can."

"You said I couldn't look into another man's eyes."

"I did. Because that would tell other doms here that you were receptive to their advances."

"I don't... I don't think I *like* to watch," I say. "I'd rather..."

"You would rather?" he prompts, eyebrow raising.

"I'd rather see you," I say. "I mean, it's hot to be here with you, while they..." I clear my throat.

Damian smirks. "You don't need to say anymore, I understand."

I relax a little, thinking it's good that he understands, because even I don't. It's not that I want anything to do with the men on stage--or the woman, for that matter. It's that being in such a sexually charged atmosphere is putting my own desires into overdrive. It feels dirty here, and not in a bad way.

Damian leans so close I think he's going to take me into his arms, but he puts his lips right next to my ear so I can hear the rasp of his whispered voice. "I'm going to make you cum right here, Kitten. Right in front of all these people."

A dirty thrill runs through me. A second later, my stomach turns over when the fear comes. What if someone turns around and sees us? What if they decide *we're* the show they want to watch?

Damian's hand meanders from my hip to my thigh, where it reverses its downward direction and moves up, this time sliding under the hem of my dress. Everywhere his touch roams leaves a fiery trail of ecstasy. I've secretly dreamt of having his hands on me like this again for so long now. Whether I realized it or not, I knew something like this would happen when I agreed to come here with him. Honestly, I knew so long as I kept agreeing to see Damian and give him chances to prove I can trust him, it was only a matter of time before I'd end up sleeping with him again.

Being around Damian is like stepping into a river with a powerful current. I can only fight the current so long before I'm swept along with it. The only way to fight it is to get out of the water all together. And I'm starting to think I'd rather drown in it than get out.

"Oh God," I gasp.

His hand finds my panties, which are embarrassingly soaked already.

"You're so wet, Kitten. Tell me, did the show get you wet? Or was it something else."

"It was you. Only you."

"Liar," he says. His finger does something I can't even begin to describe against me--something between a quick vibrating buzz and a wonderful circular motion.

The sensation is so overwhelmingly pleasurable that a moan spills out before I can bite it back. It's so loud I think someone must have heard. I scan the crowd Damian has his back to with nervous eyes. One woman has her head turned toward us now. She winks when I notice her before turning her chair to face us.

"Someone is watching us," I whisper.

"Good. That was your punishment for lying to me. Displease me, and I'll make sure you're noisy enough to draw more eyes on us."

My heartbeat grows even more rapid. I expected to be mortified at the idea of someone watching, but knowing the woman is watching us makes me imagine everything from a new, even more exciting perspective. I picture how we must look with Damian pinning me to the wall, my dress hiked up and his hand stroking my soaked panties.

He kisses my neck while his hand slips inside my panties, finding the bare skin of my pussy. He moves his hand expertly, touching me in places no man ever bothered to take the time to. His fingers move slowly down my mound, sending chills pulsing through me and making even more heat blossom in my core. His fingers eventually find my entrance and he's able to slide one finger in with ease. Even the single digit feels absolutely amazing as he curls it back and puts breathtakingly wonderful pressure on a place inside me I thought for sure was a myth.

My body bends forward involuntarily. I'm gasping into his chest now, fingers clawing into his back. "It feels so good," I moan.

"That's your g-spott," he says. "and I'm just getting started."

He somehow has the dexterity to use his thumb to circle my clit while he works a second finger into my entrance, still pumping into me and dragging his fingers along that spot that's making me delirious with pleasure. He seems to have a natural sense for how close I am to orgasm, because just when I near the edge he shifts his movements and attention just enough to keep me from climaxing.

He works a third finger inside me, still using his thumb on my clit with unbelievable skill. He pumps his hand inside me now with some kind of twisting motion that feels incredible, and when he starts to splay his fingers out every time he pulls back, my legs shake and threaten to give out.

"Oh fuck," I gasp, surprising myself. I'm not normally much of a cusser, but I'm too far along the wave of pleasure to care about manners or appearances anymore. I'm moaning louder with every thrust of his hand and movement of his thumb. I know my voice must be drawing more eyes. Right now, the idea only turns me on more. I distantly know I'll probably be mortified later, but I can't make myself stop.

I peek past Damian toward the crowd and see more than half of them are watching us with interest, and some of them are even kissing or touching each other as they watch.

I don't think Damian wanted me to cum yet, but the sight of so many people getting off on watching us combined with his fingers inside me is too much. I spasm, feeling my walls squeeze and contract around his fingers. "Oh God, Damian," I gasp, squeezing onto him like he's the only thing keeping me from being blasted away by the force of my orgasm.

When the last tremors of my pleasure have passed, he bends to pull my panties back up, then takes me by the waist and leads me toward the exit of the room with a proud expression on his face. He looks toward the crowd and *licks his fingers clean.*

I nearly have another orgasm just from the sight of it. He catches the look on my face and chuckles. "You were perfect, Kitten. Absolutely perfect."

"You weren't so bad yourself," I say.

"Sir," he corrects with surprising sternness.

"Sir," I say, lowering my head. Even though this is in many ways just a game--I don't want to disappoint him. It doesn't feel like a game when his hand is on my back and the pulsing music of this place hums in my chest. When I think I'm pleasing him, everything feels right.

"What now?" I ask. "Sir," I add hastily.

"It's time for some privacy."

He takes me down a long hallway full of doorways. I can't help thinking back to the corridor in the airport with the conference rooms. It's like we're walking through a darkened shadow of that memory now. I only hope this time doesn't end like the last.

He uses a key on a door at the end of the hall, opening up a space like nothing I've ever seen. It's dark, and the faint shape of countless devices and tools stand in shadow. Fear stabs through me. "Damian," I say, stepping back toward the door. "Yellow. This is…"

He flicks a lighter, bringing the flame alive on a candle near the door. "You're scared. I know, Kitten. I'd be worried if you weren't, frankly. We don't need to use any of this tonight if you're not ready. We can just sit in here and talk, let you get used to seeing all of this."

"Have you used everything in here?" I ask, looking around as my eyes adjust to the darkness and I can see the countless devices and tools, not to mention furniture that I can't even begin to guess the use of.

He chuckles. "No. I'll be honest with you. A hundred percent honest. I've always been drawn to… *this,*" he says, motioning around the room. "Sex never brought me any real pleasure. I thought something might be wrong with me. I eventually stumbled upon the world of BDSM. It felt right, but I never wanted a submissive for myself," he says, pulling a leather paddle from the wall and running his thumb over it thoughtfully. "I never made it past the initial phases with any women. None of them were right. *Until you.*"

"I don't want to sound ungrateful, but I still don't understand. Why me?"

He moves close and breathes in deeply through his nose. "Because you infatuate me. Your smell, your beauty, the aura of innocence that clings to you like armor. I want it all for myself, more than I've ever wanted anything. I want you. I want to be part of your life, part of your son's life. I don't even care if you never want to use a room like this. I just want you."

I put my arms around him and nuzzle my face into his chest. I can't believe how good it feels to be held by him, to be close to him. "There's something I need to tell you," I say. "Before we can go any farther with this, before… I just need to tell you." The words tumble out of me faster than I can stop, but I know I'm doing the right thing. He needs to know.

10

DAMIAN

"That day..." she pauses briefly looking unsure, but forges on. "You got me pregnant.

My stomach clenches so tightly I nearly double over. *Pregnant?* My mind is already racing to conclusions--to the one conclusion I want to believe so badly it hurts. *Is Dean mine?*

"Dean?" I ask breathlessly. I feel tears prick at my eyes but I hold them back.

She nods, watching me carefully. I realize she's scared. My kitten is scared that I'll be mad. "Yes."

"Does he know?" I ask.

"No," she says. Her eyes fill with tears.

I want to make her feel better, but despite my best efforts, I feel a swell of something dark and angry inside me. She didn't tell me. She held this from me for three years--three years of my son's life I can never get back. My fists clench at my sides and I take an involuntary step back. If I were being rational, I would remember that she didn't know me nor did she know how to locate me and she didn't have the means that I did to search for her, but right now I can't see past my anger.

"Say something," she pleads, moving toward me.

I hold up a hand, stopping her. "Just give me a second. I just need a second."

She breaks down now, tears streaming down her cheeks as she rips the door open and running back out into the club.

I want to chase after her, but my legs won't move. Nothing will move. I feel only the crushing sense of loss pushing down on me like the weight of a mountain. I missed his first steps, his first words... I missed so much.

And the first time I saw my own son? I saw him with a knife twisting in my heart because I thought Kylie had been with another man, that she had a child with another man.

I slam my fist into the wall. Fiery pain bites through me, but I let it run its course, savoring the distraction. "Fuck," I growl. In my own selfish anger, I just let Kylie walk out into the club alone and unprotected. All other thoughts die in an instant. The mother of my child is out there and some fucking asshole could be trying to put his hands on her right now.

I rush out into the hall, hurrying down the corridor and barging in every door along the way. Some are locked, but I throw my shoulder into the doors and check anyway, not caring about the angry shouts of protest that follow in my wake.

"Kylie!" I shout. "Kylie!"

I reach the lobby and still see no sign of her. Just before I run outside to check the parking lot, I take one last look over my shoulder. I barely catch sight of a tall man in a suit who has Kylie pinned in a corner. His hands aren't on her, but he's standing too close. Way too fucking close.

I'm on him in a second. I yank him around to face me by the shoulder. He's tall, but not taller than me, and he has to look up slightly to meet my eyes. "She's spoken for," I say, moving my eyes to Kylie's long enough to make sure she hears my message loud and clear. *You're still mine, Kitten. I may need to punish you for holding the truth from me, but you're still mine.*

The man has defiant eyes and an obnoxiously thick chin. It's a punchable face if I've ever seen one, and all he needs to do is give me an excuse. "Spoken for?" he says in disbelief. "By you?"

I grip his suit and lift him an inch off the ground before pressing him into the wall. He reaches to pry my hands free but doesn't have the strength.

I'm satisfied to see Kylie doesn't try to stop me. She only watches with her mouth pressed into an angry line. I just don't know if she's angry at him or me, but that's a problem for later. Right now I need to set this fucker straight.

"Did he touch you?" I ask Kylie.

"On the shoulder," she says quietly. "He touched my shoulder to get my attention."

My grip tightens and my teeth clench. "You touched my submissive. She's marked as untouchable. She's marked as claimed. And you touched her. You know what that means, don't you?"

"Fuck all those rules. My family is worth millions, asshole. I could buy this whole club if I wanted."

"It means," I say, ignoring him. "I could have you banned for life. *Or,* I could do something much more enjoyable."

I pull my arm back and punch him so hard in the face it sends him crumpling to the ground. He writhes and groans.

"Get up," I suggest. "Just give me an excuse to hit you again."

Some of the members of the club are watching us, but fights aren't uncommon, especially not here. Many clubs have extremely strict rules enforced by bouncers, but this club has always catered to an almost wild west style of justice. It's part of the charm, I guess.

He wisely stays down.

"Come on," I say to Kylie. "We need to talk."

She looks worried, but falls in beside me as we walk outside. I take her to my car and open the passenger door for her. Once I'm in the driver's seat, I let out a long sigh, searching for the right words. "I won't apologize for how I reacted," I say carefully. "But let me make myself perfectly clear. We have a child together. A son," I add, unable to stop from smiling a little at that. "You're the mother of my child. There's nothing I won't do to make sure you're mine and mine alone. *Nothing.* And now we owe it to our son to make this work. Am I angry that you held this from me? Yes. I'm fucking angry. But we'll talk about that another day when I've had the proper amount of time to think of an appropriate punishment for you."

She lowers her head, thinking for a long moment before she responds. "But do you understand why I didn't tell you? I didn't even know I was pregnant when I left three years ago. I didn't know how to find you for one thing. And then you came back into my life and I still wasn't sure if you were telling the truth or if Faleena was."

I cringe at the mention of her name. No one has earned the scary level of hatred I hold than that woman. She took more from me than she could ever know with her scheme three years ago, and now the price I paid for her jealousy is even higher.

"You should have told me when I came to your office," I say.

Kylie gives me a exasperated look. "Yeah? Oh hi, Damian! Long time no see. By the way, you knocked me up when you fucked me in that conference room in an airport three years ago. We have a son together."

My anger flares at the tone she takes. I'm cupping her chin with my hand before I realize it. "Be careful," I growl. "I'm already on edge, and you're pushing me. You don't want to push me. Not right now."

She meets my eyes defiantly. "I don't? We're not in the club anymore. I don't have to be your submissive out here."

My breath is coming rapidly and my mind is filling with ideas that have my cock stiffening in a confusing blend of anger and arousal. As much as I want her submission, I enjoy the idea of wrestling it from her just as much. "It sounds like I need to teach you a lesson, Kitten. Get in the back seat."

"No," she says.

I study her face carefully, looking for signs of arousal. Her pupils are dilated slightly. Her cheeks are flushed red. She pushes her chest out slightly, giving me a clear view of her cleavage. And most telling of all, her legs are parted just enough to let me see her white panties and the dark patch of fresh moisture staining them.

She safe worded me in the club, and I have a moment of doubt. Does she realize the safe words will still work out here? As much as I don't want to soften the experience by reminding her, I have more important things to think about than my cock now. *I'm a father.* Every time that thought skids across my consciousness it sends giddy waves of excitement through me.

"You remember the safe words?" I ask.

Momentary surprise registers on her face and she nods quickly.

"Good," I growl. "Because you have two choices. You can either get in the fucking back of the car, or I'm going to drag you out of that door and throw you in the back."

Her eyes widen. "I'm not moving," she says with a glint of excitement in her eyes.

I throw open my door, storm to her side of the car, and yank her door open. I grab her with both arms, pulling her into my chest and turning her away from the car so she won't hurt herself by accidentally kicking the car as she struggles to get free. I open the back door and throw her in, making sure she lands on the seat and doesn't hit her head on anything. I yank on a lever beneath the passenger seat that lets me fold it up and push it close enough to the dash to give me all the space I'll need.

I'm going to need all the room I can get to enjoy my kitten the way I want.

I climb in the car, watching her with predatory eyes as she backs herself up against the far door, knees up defensively. Her dress is hiked up giving me the most amazing view of her panties I can imagine, and it's all I can do not to rush this, to get my dick out and fuck her senseless right now. But I wouldn't swallow up a filet mignon in a single bite, and I'm not about to waste this opportunity by rushing through this.

"No," she says, moving back a little as I come toward her. She has nowhere to escape to... not that she really wants to get away from me.

"No isn't the magic word, Kitten," I say. My stomach clenches in fear that she might safe word me. Stopping now would be hard. Hard as hell, but I'd do it in a heartbeat. My main goal may be to make her cum as hard as she can and turn this night into as enjoyable an experience for her as I can, but I'd be lying if I said I wasn't dying to punish her before plunging my cock into her sweet warmth again. It has been way too long since I last felt her pussy clenching around my length--felt her walls stretching to accommodate my size.

I reach for her legs to press them open more but she fights me. I test my strength against her, forcing her legs open and then moving my body between them. My lower half is on the floor board, using most of the space I freed up by moving the seat.

"Fighting me only means I'm going to give it to you harder," I say through clenched teeth.

There's a hungry flash in her eyes when she deliberately pushes against me with both hands.

"Naughty, Kitten," I say, "now you lose your hands." I grab her wrists and pin them to the seat behind her, taking the seat belt and twisting it around her wrists in a way that will keep her from breaking free without my help. As much as I'm enjoying the game of breaking through her resistance, I still don't want to hurt her, so I'm careful to leave enough room for her wrists to breathe. She won't have any lasting marks from a night with me. She never will.

Her chest heaves and she still struggles against me, pushing at me with her legs and arching her body to avoid my grasp. Even though she fights me with her body, she can't mask the look in her eyes. She's practically dripping with desire. *She's hungry for this*, maybe even as hungry as me.

"You've been bad tonight," I growl, moving my mouth to the supple skin of her neck and kissing her there. I grip the hem of her dress with one hand and pull it up to her chin, exposing her white lace panties and bra. My breath catches at the sight of her perfect body stretched out for me like a prize. *My prize.* "You're fucking beautiful. Even more beautiful than I remember."

She stops struggling against me as hard, clearly enjoying the praise. *So my kitten likes to be complemented, does she?*

I unhook her bra and grip the shoulder strap on one side with both fists, yanking hard enough to pop it free so I can let it dangle from one of her arms and out of my way. Her tits drop free of the bra with a pleasant jiggle, giving me a completely clear view of her rock-hard nipples. "I've never seen breasts so perfect," I say, cupping one of her tits and taking her nipple in my mouth.

She arches her back into me, gasping while I circle the hardened nub of her nipple with my tongue.

"I knew you were submissive, but I never imagined you'd be a disobedient brat." I say in a lower tone, just before I bite with the slightest pressure on her nipple. It's enough to make her jump with surprise.

"Ow," she gasps.

"We're just getting started, Kitten. I've been keeping track of all the times you've earned a punishment, and it's going to take more than tonight to get caught up."

I use the warmth of my tongue to soothe away what can only be a slight sting from the bite. "Pleasure and pain aren't so different," I say between kisses. I give her another taste of my teeth, this time on her other breast. She jumps slightly against the pain, but it's only a moment before I have her moaning again, this time more intensely than before.

"We enjoy salty food with sweet drinks because the flavors complement one another," I say, kissing my way lower now until the scent of her pussy reaches my nose and inflames me even further. "Too much salt and it can ruin the flavor. But pair it with something sweet and you can enjoy every bite like it's the first. Every time."

I draw a slow line with my fingertip down from her clit, through her soaked folds. Without warning, I thrust two fingers inside her to the knuckle. She arches her back and cries out.

"The pain reminds your body how sweet the pleasure is," I say, capturing her swollen clit between my lips and sucking while swirling the tip of my tongue around it. She's shaking now with the need to cum. I can sense it as if it was my own orgasm--an eruption building toward the point of explosion, so close that even the gentlest touch could trigger the release.

"And..." I say, pulling my fingers from her core and taking my mouth away. "The sudden absence of either can do more than just remind you how sweet the pleasure is."

She watches me with pleading eyes. She wants to cum. She wants whatever I'll give her and she wants it so badly she can barely stop herself from begging. But that's not enough for me. I want her past that point. I want her so far gone that nothing stops her from getting on her fucking knees, begging and pleading with me for the orgasm she so desperately needs. I want her complete submission.

"Absence can enhance the pleasure... or the pain." I let my words settle around her like a cold mist, knowing every second I delay will only make what she feels next more intense. "Now we reach the point of the night where I need your trust. Your absolute, complete trust."

Her eyes are unwavering, but after a long pause, she gives the slightest nod of her head. "Okay," she says quietly.

I reach into the center console and take out a black blindfold. She watches warily until I cover her eyes and tie it off behind her head. Now I have her tied up and blind, completely in my control. I take my time admiring the sight of it, savoring the knowledge that her submission is almost totally mine now. I've spent a long time thinking of how I would break her in when I finally found her, and now's my chance.

For a time, I thought the best way would be gradual. That I should gently introduce her to my world where pain and pleasure merge into one, but I realize now that isn't the way. Kylie needs to see what heights I can bring her to, and she needs to see sooner rather than later.

I won't damage her in any way. No marks left that will be there in the morning. No emotional trauma. My tool of choice tonight will be the promise of pain undelivered, the wicked potential of the sharpened edge close enough to the skin to raise hairs.

I grab the cigarette lighter and press it into the console, letting the coiled iron wire heat until it glows red hot. I put my hand in front of it, testing the radiating heat. One second is all it takes to know something incredibly hot is close. Two seconds is too much.

"I need you to remain absolutely still. If you even flinch, you will be punished."

I take the lighter and hold it just a fingertip's distance from her stomach, careful to move it slowly but quickly enough across her bare skin to let her feel the intensity of the heat without burning her in the slightest.

Her breathing quickens, chest heaving. I have to pull the lighter back slightly to avoid it touching her as her body writhes in fear. "Remember," I say quietly, reaching to re-heat the lighter in the console. "I'm only reminding your body where the line is between pleasure and pain. I'm resetting the middle-line to a place closer to pain, so that even a breath of fresh air will feel as explosive as my fingers in your pussy. But you're going to be doing more than breathing fresh air."

I subject her to a full two minutes of the heat. I'm pleasantly surprised when she doesn't protest in the least. My kitten is proving to be a more suitable submissive than even I could have hoped after all.

"Now, something more intense," I say, unbuckling my belt as quietly as I possibly can and slipping my pants down. I pull my underwear down as well and free my throbbing cock, which is already leaking pre-cum. I want her to *think* more pain is coming. Her mind will move the needle even farther, bracing itself for pain, adjusting and adapting so she can handle the intensity by dulling it. But the same mechanism that dulls her receptiveness to pain will heighten her ability to feel pleasure. And she's about to feel a whole lot of fucking pleasure.

I grip my cock and line it up with her waiting heat, barely able to restrain myself long enough to speak. "Remember, if the pain is too intense, you know the words to make it stop." Thankfully she's blindfolded, because she can't see the grin on my face. Her fingertips dig into the seat belt and her lips quiver. She's expecting something just short of torture, and she's about to get the fastest, hardest orgasm she's ever had instead.

I ease my cock into her in a smooth, continuous motion. I don't slam it home in a way that will pinch and cause her discomfort, but I don't fuck around either. She's wet enough for me, and it's only a matter of reminding her pussy how to take a cock my size, which it seems to struggle with.

She opens her mouth in a silent exclamation of pleasure, body quivering against me and pussy clenching tighter around my cock, if that's even possible. She's so tight it's like her walls are choking my cock in the most wonderful kind of way. I can feel a tight ring of resistance around her entrance sliding over the entirety of my length with every thrust. Her pussy is so much wetter and hotter than anything I've ever felt, even more than what I remember three years ago. She's ready now. She wants this as much as I do.

"God you're so fucking wet," I say.

She makes an embarrassed face and turns away from me, still blindfolded.

"It's amazing," I say, cupping her chin and leaning down to kiss her. I've spent so long waiting for this, imagining all the ways I'd bring her under my total control. I thought of the ways I'd torturously drag out her orgasm, denying her until she's like a puddle at my feet, helpless and desperate for the final touch that would put her over the edge.

But now?

I can't stop. My body grinds into her, each thrust of my hips driving heavy breaths from my lungs. My entire body tingles with the unstoppable current of my orgasm that is getting closer by the second. I wanted this to be entirely about her. I didn't think my own needs would even factor in until I decided to let them.

I forgot what it was like to be with her. She's not like the others. Not in the slightest.

"I want to see you," she gasps. "Let me--*ohh*--let me see you."

I rip the blindfold from her head, not realizing how much I want to see her heavy eyes looking back up at me. I'm overcome by a sudden urge to have her completely free, so I tug the seat belt away from her wrists too. She hooks her leg around me and turns me so that I'm sitting on the seat and she's on top of me, straddling me with my cock still buried inside her. She puts one arm behind my neck and places the other on my cheek. Our eyes never waver from each other as our bodies move together in perfect sync.

At some point it stops becoming just sex. It's not my cock in her pussy or anything so simple. Every time she gyrates her hips and fills herself with me, I see the change slowly coming into her eyes. I grip her waist, using her like a fuck doll until our bodies are practically a blur of motion, until the sensation of her pussy gripping me is a singular, explosive wave that rocks me from my toes to my fingertips. Everything fades away. The condensation gathering on the windows, the handprint she left when she flipped over and started riding me, the anger I felt for her holding the truth about Dean back from me. It's all gone. There's only us. This moment.

I don't want it to stop, but when she takes my hand and sucks my thumb into her mouth, swirling her hot little tongue around my finger and pulling it out of her full lips, I'm undone.

My body tenses and my grip on her waist must be painful by now as I slam her body down onto me again and again, using her pussy as my cock pulses with what seems like an orgasm that has no end.

She wraps her arms around my neck, body going rigid and shaking when her own orgasm comes. Her walls tense around me in waves, drawing every last drop of cum from my cock deep into her core.

"Fuck," I roar.

"Damian," she half-whimpers, muffling her own moans when she bends to kiss me.

I lose track of how long we lay together in the back of my car with the windows fogged. It's only when Kylie finally sits up and pulls her dress back down that I'm able to think straight again. My mind goes straight to Dean. *My son.*

"When can I see him?" I ask.

"Dean?" she asks. "He'll be asleep tonight, but you could come by tomorrow. Just... I don't know if it's a good idea to tell him the truth right away."

My jaw clenches. "He needs to know."

"I know, and we'll tell him. I'm only saying I want to make sure we tell him the right way. Maybe... maybe you could take us out somewhere, let him get to know you a little bit. Then we could plan out how to tell him?."

I know what she's saying is reasonable, but all I can think is how badly I want my son to know who I am. *Fuck*. I want to hold him. I want to be in his life so I can start making up for all the time I've lost. But she's right. We need to make sure we tell him the right way.

11

KYLIE

The next morning, Angie sets down a plate of eggs for me at the kitchen table.

"You really don't have to cook for me," I say with a chuckle.

"I enjoy it," she says. "Besides, tomorrow is my last day working for you, and I wanted you to try my famous scrambled eggs before I go."

I take a bite, raising my eyebrows in pleasant surprise at the tangy flavor she managed to work into them. "These are incredible."

She smiles proudly. "Sharp cheddar cheese, butter, and I add a scoop of sour cream right at the end. Best eggs you'll ever have."

I can't disagree, and even Dean is pounding his down. He's apparently in such a hurry to get the eggs in his mouth that he tossed his fork aside and is using his hands like grubby little egg shovels.

"He never eats my eggs," I say a little sourly.

Angie laughs. "Well, now you know the secret. So maybe you'll trade me a secret for a secret. *You're glowing,*" she says with a knowing smile. "The date went well last night?"

I blush furiously because the first images that come to my mind are of Damian fingering me in a room full of people while a woman on stage is getting gang-banged. If anybody knew exactly what I did last night, I'd be mortified. But I guess Melina is going to find out. She'll smell how juicy my secrets are from a mile away and dig them out of me like a bloodhound. Angie doesn't have to know all the gory details, at least.

"It went well," I say carefully. "I think I'll be seeing more of him."

Angie barks out an amused laugh. "I see. It was that good?"

My blush deepens. "Yes."

"Good," mutters Dean between mouthfuls of egg. "Neenie Good," he says, patting his shirt with his hand and smearing egg everywhere. Neenie is as close as he can come to saying Deanie, which I call him all the time.

"Yes you are good, Deanie," I say with a smile.

There's a knock at the door that makes me jump. I haven't even gotten ready yet, and I don't know who would be bugging us so early, except Damian. We didn't agree on a time, but for some reason I assumed he'd be coming by in the evening.

I make a quick and futile attempt to fix the mess that is my hair. I'm wearing saggy pajama bottoms and a white tank top that's a little big. I haven't even looked in the mirror. I briefly consider just running. Maybe if I barricaded myself in the bathroom I'd have a chance to get presentable before Damian had to see what the real me looks like. Even looking like a hot mess, I want to see him though. I can't stop myself from moving to the door and pulling it open.

My heart sinks and tightens with fear at the same time.

Melina stands in the doorway with a slightly crazed look in her eyes. She doesn't appear to have spent much time getting ready either.

"Kylie," she says in a measured voice as she lets herself in, brushing past me.

"Melina?" I ask, more than a little confused. I close the door and follow after her as she walks around my place, inspecting everything like she's expecting to find a smoking gun somewhere.

"You'll have to excuse us for a few minutes," she says to Angie, who looks as confused as me. "Kylie has to come to the bedroom with me."

Angie raises an eyebrow so high at that I think it might disappear into her hairline.

"She doesn't mean like that," I blurt, but Melina is already dragging me toward the bedroom with no signs of slowing down.

Once I'm inside, she slams the door behind us and rounds on me. "You didn't call me? Do you know how long I stayed up last night?"

Judging from the dark circles under her eyes, she stayed up late, maybe all night. "I didn't want to wake you--"

Melina slaps me across the face. It's almost playful, but it does sting a little.

I burst out laughing. "You are ridiculous."

The corner of her mouth pulls up in the faintest smirk. "You're not leaving this room until you give me details. All the details. I want to know how many buttons his suit had, how he did his hair, what the place you went to was like, *how big his cock is*," she adds under her breath.

"Melina!" I say, still laughing.

It takes less time than I would've thought to fill Melina in on everything, except one part. I don't tell her about Dean, or what happened between Damian and I three years ago. I hoped she wouldn't press me for more details, but she's watching me now that I'm done, eyes narrowed suspiciously.

"I don't get it," she says. "You went into the crazy torture room, then you just ran away? Why did you leave?"

I look to to the side, pulling at my fingers while I try to think of a convincing lie, except I've never made a habit of lying to Melina, and I don't really want to start now. She's a good friend.

She always has been, and she doesn't deserve to be lied to. Maybe I've withheld the truth from her about Damian from the start, but there's a big difference between not offering up the truth and lying when asked a direct question.

"I knew Damian before he came into the office," I say slowly. "Like, three years before. We kind of had a one night stand. In an airport."

"So what now? Are you lovebirds going to tie the knot or something?

I laugh. "I'd be lying if I said the thought never crossed my mind. But marriage? You saw him, right? Can you picture a man like Damian scrambling eggs for the family in the morning, changing diapers, or helping sweep the floors?"

Melina looks thoughtfully toward the ceiling and grins, eyebrows rising. "Naked. Yes, I can picture him doing all that. *Naked,"* she adds again.

"You know, if you keep drooling over him, we may have to throw down," I say.

Melina gives me an amused look. "Please don't tempt me. The idea of you trying to fight is so hilarious I might just have to provoke you so I can see it."

I feel an unexpected surge of annoyance. "I'm serious. You have your own man. All the little jokes about Damian you've been making need to stop."

The humor slips from her face a little as she watches me. "You're really going to get pissy with me over some jokes?"

My nostrils flare. I don't know what's coming over me. I've never been the raging, jealous girlfriend type--if I even qualify as his girlfriend, that is. But right now Melina is pressing all the wrong buttons. She thinks she doesn't need to be afraid of me? She might be more scared when she's got my handprint on her face. "I'm not getting *pissy*. I just don't want you joking about seeing my boyfriend naked. Or any of the other sexual stuff you've said."

"Your boyfriend, is he?" she teases.

"Stop it," I say, pushing her.

She looks down at where my hands touched her with wide eyes. "You actually pushed me." she says.

"Yeah, and I'll do more than that if you don't stop being a creep."

I'm already feeling a little silly for losing my temper so quickly. I'm about to apologize and blow it off when Melina scares the living crap out of me by yelling out a war-cry and charging me. She catches my chest with her shoulder, driving me onto the bed, where she begins tickle attacking me. I've always been ticklish, and she knows it.

Within seconds, I'm kicking, laughing, and trying to tickle her back but none of it is working.

"Think you're so tough?" she asks with a grin. "Think you can boss me around? Not as long as you're this ticklish, bitch."

I laugh, holding my stomach both to protect myself and massage my sides, which already hurt from laughing.

The door opens. We both freeze--with Melina straddling me and her hands just beneath my boobs and my own hands near my belly.

"Am I interrupting?" asks Damian.

I briefly imagine how this must look from his perspective and blush so much that my cheeks hurt. "I'm ticklish..." I say in a small voice, as if that is anything close to an explanation.

"Good to know," says Damian. "I'll remember that next time you misbehave."

Melina looks at me with her back to Damian and mouths "*Oh my God.*"

I give her a quick look that I hope conveys a very clear message: *Don't be weird.* Well, it's too late for that one I guess, but I push her off me.

"If you could give us a minute?" says Damian.

Melina looks at him defiantly, planting a hand on her hip.

"Whatever you have to say to her, you can say in front of me."

"Melina," I say sternly.

She gives me a sideways glance but doesn't budge.

Damian clears his throat. Despite all her tough talk, it only takes one look from Damian to have her practically scurrying out of the room and closing the door.

"Should I be worried?" he asks with a half-grin.

"No," I say. "No. Absolutely not. Melina is just... *special*. She's protective too. Like a misguided chihuahua."

"Hmm," he says. "I was hoping to take you and Dean out for a little fun. Will I have to run that through your bodyguard?"

"Somehow, I think we'll be able to get past her."

When we leave my bedroom, Melina nearly falls into us. She straightens awkwardly, brushing imaginary wrinkles from her shirt, then makes a poor attempt of looking innocent. "You know I think you may have termite damage in this doorframe," she says.

"You weasel," I say. "You were listening in?"

"No. But if I was, I'd tell you I'm way cuter and prettier than a freaking chihuahua."

Damian gives me a sideways glance.

"I know she's out of control," I say. "But she's got a certain kind of charm. Once you get used to her."

"I see," says Damian. "Well, I can't wait until that happens."

"Hey," says Melina indignantly. "Maybe you should speak for yourself."

He raises a dangerous eyebrow at her that has her shrinking back.

Dean bursts into the living room wearing nothing but a pair of little brown sandals and his training pants. "Nakie, nakie!" he shouts proudly.

Angie comes out of the kitchen, assesses the situation, and makes a surprisingly athletic lunge for Dean, but he's too fast. He ducks her arms and spins free, stomping and clapping with joy at having evaded capture. Melina makes a half-hearted attempt to wrangle him when he comes her way, but he weaves between her legs.

"Nakie, nakie!" He laughs gleefully.

Like a bullfighter, I snag his favorite blanket and wave it where he can see it, hoping to lure him into my reach, but he's wise to my tricks too, and he makes a wide turn around me.

Damian takes a casual step forward, reaches, and wraps Dean up in his arms. Dean struggles at first, but once Damian unleashes a flurry of tickles, all Dean can do is wiggle and laugh in Damian's arms.

I watch the two of them closely, my heart thudding when I realize the significance. It's the first time Damian has knowingly held his own son. And every single doubt I could've possibly had about bringing him into our lives is blasted away the moment I see the way Damian looks at Dean. Dean is none the wiser to it, laughing with his head back and his little hands clasping at Damian's.

There's a sparkle in Damian's eye, and if I didn't know better, I'd say he was on the verge of tearing up. When he's done tickling Dean, he pulls him into a hug, closing his eyes tight and taking a deep breath. I expect Dean to wiggle away because he's at the age where he's got too much he wants to do to be bothered with long hugs, but Dean doesn't budge. He even leans his head into Damian's shoulder and puts his arms around him.

My throat tightens and my eyes fill with tears. I slip back into my bedroom and press my back to the wall, sinking down and crying. I'm crying not just because I can see how perfect Damian is going to be with Dean, but because I played a huge part in keeping him away from Dean until now. Even if I thought I had good reasons to leave, and even if I had no way of knowing I was pregnant when I left, I knew Damian had to be the father when I found out I was pregnant. Trusting what Faleena told me about him was a mistake I'm going to have to live with for the rest of my life, and I only hope I've been a good enough mom to Dean on my own to make up for the gaping absence of a father.

But it's going to change now. It's all going to change. Whether I made a mistake in the past or not, Damian really meant everything he said. He wants to be with me. He wants to be part of Dean's life. He wants to take care of us.

I feel so much relief and joy from that knowledge it almost scares me. No matter how much I may feel like I know Damian, the fact remains that I've spent less than a week with him in total. A few hours at the airport three years ago. A little bit of time at the party I went to with Alec and Melina. A few minutes in the office. Our dinner date. Then last night at the club. And now this... Just snapshots. I have nothing more than snapshots of this man, yet I feel like I know him. I feel like I can *trust* him.

Maybe that's crazy. I just hope like hell it's not, because I don't think I can stop feeling the way I do.

"He's the father, isn't he?" asks Melina, who slips into my room and closes the door quietly behind her.

I wipe my eyes and sniffle. "Yes." Admitting it feels better than it should, like I just dropped a weight I'd been carrying for so long I stopped noticing, only now that it's gone I feel the relief surging through me. "Yes," I say again. "It's a long story, and I'll tell you later. I promise. But yes."

Melina kneels beside me and gives me a long, tight hug. "Good," she says. "And whatever it is you seem to think you did wrong," she adds, wiping another tear from my eye. "I'm going to need you to stop blaming yourself. I know you. I know you'd only ever do what you thought was best for Dean. So whatever it is that got you here, don't play 'what if.' Just accept it. You made those decisions and now you're here for a reason."

"How do you manage to give relevant advice when you have no idea what's going on?" I ask.

"I've always been pretty awesome."

I laugh. I take a deep breath, wiping my eyes. "Do I

look okay?"

"You look like you were just crying, but it's okay. I told him you get really bad allergies sometimes and I was going to come make sure you had your medicine."

"Great, now he's going to be wondering why I am miraculously cured of allergies after today."

"One problem at a time, chicka."

I roll my eyes. "Unless you're here. Then it's like twelve problems per minute."

"Ungrateful little..." she mutters with a grin. "Why don't you go out there and let the man sweep you off your feet before I decide to pop you right in the kisser."

I scrunch up my nose. "Pop me right in the kisser? What are you, some gangster from the 80s?"

"No. I'm your best friend who loves you and wants to see you happy for once. *Really happy.* And I'm also the friend who is going to pop your right in the kisser if you leave that gorgeous man waiting any longer."

I smile and give her a quick hug before heading back into the living room.

"Everything okay?" he asks, moving to take me by the shoulders and inspect me, like he's expecting to see a wound somewhere. His eyes linger for a long time on mine, which are likely a little red and swollen from the brief crying jag that I had. "Melina said you had allergies, but I never noticed any symptoms before. So I was worried."

A few days ago, I would've lied and told him it was fine. I would've just played it off and taken the easy out Melina gave me. But if I felt like I had a right to make Damian jump through hoops to prove I could trust him, I also can't let myself start lying to him. "Seeing you two together was really special," I say. "That's all. I didn't expect it to hit me so hard but it did."

He kisses my forehead, which prompts Dean to start making kissing noises as he hugs my leg. I know Angie and Melina are watching us and I feel all kinds of awkward having a moment like this in front of them, but somehow I can't make myself care. Maybe it's a new me. A version of myself that isn't always trying to hide my emotions and just shrug things off. A me that doesn't let worries about what people will think get in the way of really living. Whatever it is, I like it, because I know exactly what the old me would've done. She would've cleared her throat uncomfortably and excused herself from the situation.

Now?

I thread my fingers through Damian's hair and pull him down so I can kiss his lips. "I love you," I say. "I don't care anymore if that's crazy. I feel like I know you better than anyone I've ever known in my life, and I love you."

My chest thumps with the rapid beats of my heart, breasts rising and falling as I suck in expectant breaths. *Did I really just drop the "L" bomb after what was basically just one real date?* He's going to think I'm crazy. One-hundred percent, absolutely cra--

"I love you too," he says.

Each word spikes through me like something visceral, so thick and rich with happiness I can actually feel the emotion blossoming through my body and leaving warmth in its wake. Damian has made it no secret that he cares about me and wants me to be his since he came back. He's possessive and determined as hell. I knew all that. But love? Love is a completely different idea, and until I blundered and blurted my way to professing my premature love for him, I was pretty sure he was more of a lust kind of guy than a love kind of guy.

"Yay!" says Melina. She claps a few quick times before realizing it's not exactly the moment for it. "I actually have to pee," she says quietly before excusing herself.

Angie just winks at me and turns back to the dishes. Dean has absolutely no idea what's going on, but he is tugging at Damian's leg, wanting to be held.

"So," I say. "About that date..."

12

DAMIAN

"Ice skating?" Kylie asks. "Why is this place so deserted?

"I pulled a few strings. I figure Dean is probably too young to really nail the skating part, so..." I nod my head at the kid I spoke to over the phone, who comes out from the concession stand with a big black garbage bag over his shoulder. He lays it at our feet. "Just like you asked, sir."

"Great," I say, sliding a few hundreds into the kid's hands. He looks at the money with wide eyes. "Now go man the DJ booth."

He nods rapidly, running so fast toward the booth that he nearly falls over several times.

Kylie frowns at me in confusion. Dean is already squatting in front of the bag, grabbing it with both hands, and shaking it up and down while he giggles.

I kneel beside him. "Look at *this*," I say, opening the bag and pulling out the costumes. One is a huge elephant costume big enough for Kylie. The other is the lion in my size. The smallest is a panda bear small enough for Dean. His eyebrows come down as he takes in the costumes. With a hilariously high pitched voice, he does a convincing imitation of a lion's roar.

"That's good," I say, raising my eyebrows at Kylie.

She smirks. "He can do an elephant too."

Right on cue, Dean blows out a raspberry that sounds a little like an elephant.

"This is adorable," she says. "I can't believe you thought of this."

"They are pretty heavily padded, and I had them put a helmet inside the panda head for Dean, so he should be able to just fall and roll around as much as he wants without getting hurt. Think he'll like that?"

Kylie nods. "Oh yeah. We may not ever be able to get him to leave."

A few minutes later, the three of us are all skating on the empty ice rink to the sound of *Staying Alive,* by the Bee Gee's. The skating rink had training skates for Dean, which have two little wheels set out wide from the blade to help him keep his balance. But Dean is having more fun crashing on purpose than actually trying to stay upright.

Kylie lets out a terrified scream when Dean sets his sights on her. He sets his course for a slow but inevitable collision, and Kylie can only watch as the little panda comes inching toward her. He actually lowers his head at the last minute and does his little version of a bear's roar. Kylie throws herself back, bouncing harmlessly off the ice in her thick elephant costume. It's so thick around the middle that she can't get up without my help. I help Dean up first, which turns out to be a mistake because he mercilessly headbutts me next. I have no choice but to hit the ice right beside Kylie, roaring in mock pain.

"Oh no!" says Dean. "Boo boo!" he is tipped over too, so he can only wiggle and kick his legs uselessly to try to get closer to me to help my imagined injury.

It's nearly five minutes before I manage to get all of us on our feet again. Dean gets distracted when he realizes he can skate into the wall and bounce off, which gives me a minute alone with Kylie.

We're both breathless and smiling when we take off our masks.

"I would've never thought of something like this," Kylie says.

"That's what I'm here for."

The look on her face grows more serious. "I'm sorry it took so long. I should have tried to look for you. I'm sorry that you had to miss so much."

I shake my head. "Don't be. I'm just worried about making the most of right now. We can't change what happened, but we can focus on making every day the best it can be for him. *For us.*"

She tries to hug me, but the bellies of our costumes make us bounce apart. I barely keep my balance, but Kylie falls on her butt. I'm about to offer her my hand when a commotion draws my attention. I quickly help her up and we both watch the swarm of costumed moms and toddlers come storming in through the front doors.

"What the..." starts Kylie

"Sorry, I forgot to tell you. I thought it would be more fun for Dean if there were some other kids for him to ram into. I reached out to a local mom's group and told them everything would be paid for. I guess there was some interest."

"Yeah, no kidding."

Before long, there are at least twenty other toddlers in various costumes, all bumping and bouncing around the rink. The entire place is filled with old disco music and the high-pitched laughter of kids. Most of the moms are costumed as well, skating around and helping to police the kids. I nod to Angie, who I secretly got to agree to come keep an eye on Dean so Kylie could have a chance to relax and enjoy herself.

We eventually move outside the skating area to catch our breath and grab some nachos from the concession stand.

"You're just full of surprises, aren't you?" she asks while we share the nachos and watch the kids have a blast. "On one hand you're Mr. Dominant McPunisher, and on the other you're pretty much the perfect dad."

"Dad," I say slowly, testing the way it feels to say it out loud. "I guess I am a dad, aren't I?"

"You are," she says seriously. "And you're already making a really good case for dad of the year."

"It's hard to take you seriously when you're wearing an elephant costume," I say with a grin.

She looks down and clutches the paunch of her costume, shaking it around playfully. "You aren't turned on?"

I slide my hand behind her, gripping what I can of her ass through the thick costume. "You could wear a garbage bag and still turn me on, Kitten."

I love watching the way I can affect her. The simple touch and a few carefully chosen words and I can already see the hairs rising on the back of her neck. I know her pussy is heating for me, and I know I could have her wet enough to fuck in just seconds if I wanted to. But now clearly isn't the time.

"Damian Price?" asks a woman I didn't notice approaching us. She's one of the few people in the entire building not wearing a costume. She wears her blonde hair in a tight bun and her clothes are even tighter. I recognize her immediately as one of the reporters who was always hounding me a few years back when it got out that I was dating Faleena.

"We're trying to enjoy ourselves," I say.

"Want to introduce me to your friend?" she asks, holding her phone up in a poor attempt at discretion.

"No," I say. "I want you to give us some privacy."

"Who is this?" asks Kylie.

"Privacy?" asks the reporter. "I can see why a beautiful couple like yourselves would want privacy. By the way, I notice your son bears a striking similarity to Mr. Price. Do you care to comment?" she asks Kylie.

I stand up, push her phone away, and place my body between her and Kylie. "You need to leave."

She makes an expression that doesn't look all-too-concerned and turns to leave. "We'll be in touch."

"No," I growl. "We won't."

Once she leaves, Kylie looks at me with worry creasing her forehead. "What was that about?"

"She's from one of those trashy gossip magazines. Don't worry about her."

"Gossip magazine? You mean like the kind that are in the checkout aisles at the grocery store?"

"Yeah, I guess."

"Don't worry about her? What if our faces end up plastered all over those things? What if *Dean* ends up on one?"

I grit my teeth. "I'll do everything in my power to stop that from happening."

Kylie looks toward Dean, who is in the middle of a pile of costumed toddlers who are all rolling around on the ice. "I hope so."

13
_____

KYLIE

"Oh my God," says Melina, who leans back in her chair by my desk during Steve's extended break. "That sounds so fun. I can't believe he thought of such a cute date idea."

"I know," I say, smiling a little too proudly. It's hard not to be proud of Damian, though. As much as I don't want to think of him like some kind of prize, he really is. He's gorgeous, kind, great with Dean, and when he wants to turn me on he's like a sex god. He also has more money than he could ever spend in a single lifetime, but that doesn't even matter. Sure, it's nice, but Damian could be even more poor than me and I'd still be head-over-heels for him. The money is just a crazy bonus, like hot fudge on a brownie. "But there was this reporter who hassled us a little yesterday. It was really weird. I felt like some celebrity with the paparazzi coming after me."

"Sounds kind of exciting," she says.

"Maybe if I didn't have Dean. But she was clearly digging for dirt, or at the least something sensational and juicy. I don't want my little guy dragged into that."

"Yeah," says Melina with a frown. "What did Damian say about it?"

"It sounded like he had seen the woman before. He said he'd do anything he could to make sure it didn't go any farther."

"He knew her? Was she pretty?" asks Melina.

I feel a stab of ugly panic shoot through me. I hadn't even thought of it like that, but Melina's question makes all kinds of dark thoughts bounce around my head. "She was beautiful," I say. "And she was dressed like she knew it."

Melina's frown deepens. "How did Damian seem with her?"

"I mean, he seemed pissed. His eyes didn't wander at all or anything, and he basically told her to fuck off."

Melina relaxes. "Pshh. You have nothing to worry about. I shouldn't even be bringing stuff like that up. Your man is perfect, Kylie. He knows he's got something special with you and he's not going to do anything to jeopardize it."

"Yeah," I say, but as much as I want to trust him one hundred percent, there's the smallest, tiniest sliver of doubt that still remains. If I hadn't had three years to stew over what I thought was the truth about him, I'm sure I would've moved past this silly thing by now, but no matter how hard I try there's the faintest fear in my chest, like Damian will really do *anything* to get this woman to leave us alone.

"Wow," I say later that night when Damian leads me into a posh little bar near the center of the city. "I thought you had to have a reservation months ahead of time to get into this place."

"I worked out a deal with the owner a few years back. He owed me a couple favors."

I purse my lips. "I guess I shouldn't be surprised. Thank you by the way for paying to have Angie stay with Dean tonight while he sleeps."

"Don't thank me. It was more of a selfish decision than

anything. I'm hoping if I play my cards right tonight, I may get lucky."

I laugh, but decide to keep him on his toes at least a little. "We'll see how it goes."

He eyes me as we're let in through the front entrance by two men in dark suits. "Well, I hope you remember the safe words."

My eyes widen when I realize the inside of the club is absolutely decked out with BDSM gear. Whips, chains, and leather harnesses dangle from the walls. Full-body leather suits are on display by mannequins, and there are several areas lit by red spotlights where masked men and women are engaged in everything from intercourse to paddling. The clientele are dressed in business formal attire, but it doesn't take much searching to find men with hands up women's dresses, women with their hands inside men's zippers, and even one man who is practically swallowed up by four writhing women in a corner near where the people under the red spotlights are having sex.

"I remember them, *Sir,*" I add at the last second.

"That's good, Kitten," he says. I can already see the change coming over him, like the energy of this place seeps into him and pushes all the carefree kindness I've come to know in him away. All that's left is his primal urge to dominate and subdue, to make me his and to own me completely.

I wondered for the longest time how a relationship would work with a man like him, especially a man who has such exotic sexual tastes, but I think I finally understand. Just because he's my dom, it doesn't mean he has to be my dom at home or around Dean. He can turn it on and off like the flip of a switch, just like most couples turn their sexuality on and off. Maybe there are a few whispered words here and there or discreet touches, but every couple holds their sexuality at bay to a degree. The only difference here is the intensity of what he unleashes when the time comes.

"I still haven't had a chance to properly punish you for all of your transgressions," he explains. "I have my own personal room here, so I thought--"

"Damian," says a man who comes to clap Damian on the shoulder. The man is flanked by two gorgeous women in leather outfits that are cut like one-piece swimsuits. They both wear severe, thigh-high boots decked out with metal clasps and leather straps. "It's good to see you. It has certainly been a while."

"Kitten," he says, pulling me close to him. "This is Mark, an old business associate."

"Oh come on," says Mark, who has handsome features with flecks of gray in his hair. "Business associate? We were practically inseparable back in our hay day."

"That's enough," says Damian sharply.

Mark eyes me knowingly and grins. "I see. You're breaking in a new one, are you? Well, don't let me spoil the fun. Come on girls, I got a strap on for you this weekend, Vanessa, and I want to watch you fuck Mindy." He throws a wink at me over his shoulder as he leaves.

I look up to Damian, a dozen questions burning on the tip of my tongue. I know I'm not supposed to ask him questions right now, but I don't know if I can hold them back. Why was Damian so quick to get Mark to stop talking? What was Mark about to say that Damian didn't want me to know? Between the reporter yesterday and now this, the confident foundation of trust I've been building with Damian feels like it is being shaken, and that realization makes me sick to my stomach.

He looks down at me, and if I didn't know better, I'd say he was waiting to see if I was going to ask.

I want to ask him so badly it actually hurts, but I don't. On one hand, I need to be a better person than I was three years ago. I need to give him a chance to make the truth clear to me instead of trusting a stranger. On the other hand, I want to know if he'll come clean with whatever it is. If I can really trust Damian, I won't need to be on the alert all the time. I don't need to be his interrogator. If it's important for me to know, I need to trust him to tell me. And if he chooses not to tell me, well, I need to trust that he's making that decision for a good reason, too.

I think I see a flicker of pride in his eyes when I stay silent. His approval makes me swell with satisfaction at having pleased him. My curiosity still stings, but I can manage it. Knowing I've made Damian--*my dom*--happy is enough to distract me for now.

"Do you mind if I just use the bathroom?" I ask.

"Of course," he says, motioning to an area near the back of the main room.

I step inside to a relatively crowded space with a few well-kept stalls and a small mob of beautiful women checking themselves in the mirror and touching up makeup. Once I've finished, I'm met outside the stall by a face I don't immediately recognize. She's clearly waiting for me though, with fists planted on her shapely hips and a wicked grin on her lips.

"We never properly met," she says, extending a hand.

I shake it, even though my impulse is to slap it away. It's the reporter from yesterday, and just the sight of her alone is enough to turn my stomach. "I'm Kylie," I say. I'll give her a chance, at least. When I used to wait tables I learned the best way to deal with people I didn't like was to kill them with kindness. Maybe that'll work with this woman.

"Monique," she says.

"You just happened to be here tonight?" I say lightly. "That's a pretty wild coincidence, huh?"

She shrugs. "It was intentional. I wanted a chance to have a word with you alone, and my work affords me a few helpful perks, like being able to get into this club."

"So you're... into all this?" I ask.

"I had better be, or I would've never survived dating Damian. Oh," she says at the expression on my face. "He didn't mention we dated? I guess that's not a surprise. I think there might have been a little overlap. He only broke things off with me... what was it, yesterday? Two days ago?"

I feel like I might be sick, but I don't want her to see. "That can't be true."

She laughs with a heavy hint of sarcasm. "I know, right? I thought the same thing when he broke it off with me. But hey, now you know and you'll be better off without him. He's just a player. Always will be. You're pretty enough, anyway. You'll find another guy."

"I have to go," I say stiffly, pushing past her and heading for the exit. My head is spinning. I keep thinking how much this feels like what I felt on that airplane three years ago, only it's worse now. I let myself fall farther for him. I let it all get deeper. *I let him into Dean's life.*

I close my eyes, pressing my body against the wall and suppressing a shiver. There's a difference though. Last time I believed Faleena. I believed every word she said and I didn't even speak to Damian before I ran. This time? I may be pissed, and I may be having trouble ignoring everything she said, but I'm going to talk to him. I've changed at least that much, and the trust we've built over the past days has to count for something.

I hope.

Damian finds me before I move away from the wall. He plants a hand beside my head, leaning down and tilting my chin up with his other hand. "What happened?" he asks with eyes full of darkness.

"I met Monique," I say. "She said you two dated."

Damian shakes his head. "No. She tried when she first started reporting on me, but nothing ever happened."

"She said you were dating her until just a few days ago..."

Damian frowns in genuine confusion, and before he even says a word, I know the truth. She was lying. Every word of it was a lie. She's jealous of me, and she wants to sabotage what we have. All the disappointment and sadness I felt boils over into a simmering hatred for that woman.

The door beside us opens and Monique comes strutting out, looking pleased with herself.

Damian moves like he's about to stop her and say something, but I beat him to it.

"Hey," I say through gritted teeth, grabbing her shoulder.

She turns with a look of outrage on her face.

I don't even let her speak before I slap her as hard as I can across the face. The sound rings out but doesn't even draw so much as a turned head, which I guess isn't surprising since there's literally a guy in a leather mask spanking a bare-assed woman with a paddle a few feet away. But I relish in watching Monique's head snap to the side and the way she brings a shaking hand up to the spot on her cheek that's already turning red.

"You bitch," she says. She raises her hand to slap me back, but Damian is there as quick as a cat, gripping her wrist and stopping her from touching me.

"You need to leave," he says. "For good."

"Damian," she says. All the hardness melts from her face and she suddenly looks like a stray dog caught in the rain, desperate and hungry. "Please. I could be so good to you. Better than her. You *need* me. Just--"

"*Leave*," he says more forcefully.

The anger flashes back into her features as quickly as it came. "Fuck you, then. You don't deserve me."

She storms out of the club with loud clicks of her heels and Damian doesn't so much as glance back at her. "Are you okay, Kitten?" he asks.

"Thanks to you," I say.

He still runs his hands over me, checking me for marks or damage. "I'm sorry that happened. I have no fucking idea how she managed to get in here, either, but I'm going to have words with the owner about it."

"It's okay, really."

He watches me for a long time, then bites his lip. "You came to me this time. You didn't run."

I lean into him, running my fingers over his hard body with closed eyes. "I may be stubborn, but I can change."

"You can always come to me, Kitten. Always. And I'll always tell you the truth."

My roaming hands and the soothing sound of his voice are doing all the right things to me. Feeling what we have threatened makes me want him more than ever. It makes me hungry. I slide my hand down his back and grip his tight ass, grinning into his chest as I do.

"Careful," he says in a low raspy voice. "If you want to make it to the privacy of my room before I fuck you, it might be a bad idea to keep feeling me up like that."

"Noted," I say. "Then you had better hurry, because I don't think I can help myself."

He smirks. In a lightning quick move, he picks me up and presses me to his body, carrying me toward the back of the main room as easily as if I'm weightless. We pass a group of men and women who gives us a quick, drunken round of applause and cheer. I hide my face in Damian's shoulder, still not used to the idea of strangers knowing I'm about to have sex just a few rooms away. Even so, the exposure heightens my desire more. It's dirty, and it's something I never would've thought I'd be into, but I can't deny the way pulses of heat are running through my body, making my hairs stand on end.

"I want you to fuck me," I whisper in his ear. "I want it so bad."

His pace quickens at my words. He fumbles with the key for the locked door near the end of the hallway, but drops the key in his rush. "Fucking..." he growls before stepping back, gripping me tighter, and then kicking the door in.

"Wow," I say. "Should I be flattered?"

"No," he says. "You should be wet."

I chew on the side of my lip. "One step ahead of you there."

He drags a heavy bench in front of the door to keep anyone from barging in on us and turns on me with a dangerous look in his eyes.

I barely have time to take in the room, which is elegant and classy, yet clearly designed to be a BDSM enthusiast's playground.

"It's time I truly break you in, Kitten. Get on your fucking knees."

His words are so forceful that they might as well be a whip. The power of each syllable drives me down to my hands and knees. My dress rides up, exposing my wet panties to the slight chill in the air. I reach to pull the dress down, but he lunges forward, gripping my wrist so tightly it almost hurts. "You're mine now. You will do what I say and only what I say, or you'll pay the consequences. Am I clear?"

I nod, eyes darting to the outline of his huge cock straining against his pants.

He doesn't fail to notice my wandering eyes and chuckles. "My slutty little kitten is hungry for cock, is she? The only way you get what you want is if you follow my orders perfectly."

I would think being called a slut would piss me off, but it only turns me on more. It makes me feel dirty and sexy at the same time, and Damian is making me realize I enjoy both of those things very much.

"What do you want me to do?" I ask.

He half-smiles. "First, you're going to show me how wet you are for me. Turn around."

I do as he says, moving on my hands and knees so my ass is facing him.

He sucks in a breath. I hear his footsteps approach and feel him inches from me, kneeling in front of my ass. "Beautiful. Absolutely beautiful."

He runs his fingers across my pussy, nearly knocking me forward with how strongly my body reacts to his touch. I hear him lick his fingers clean and another wave of arousal explodes through me. My core throbs with need, but I know he's not going to give me what I want. Not yet. The anticipation hangs in the air so thickly I can almost feel it.

"Now. I want you to touch yourself for me. Touch yourself like you do when you're alone. Show me how you like to rub your pussy, how many fingers you like to slip into your tight little hole. And while you do it, I want you to imagine the things I'm going to do to you."

I tentatively move my hand between my legs, shifting my weight to my other hand to hold myself up as I rub myself through my panties.

"I want your panties off," he says sternly.

I slide them down to my knees, but before I can kick them all the way off he stops me.

"No. Leave them around your knees. Just like that."

A shiver runs through me. My pussy and ass are on full display for him, and the way he's orchestrating everything makes me feel so sexy, like I'm a cherished toy he's enjoying, like he has imagined all the ways he would want me and he's making them a reality. I bring my fingers back to circle around the hood of my clit lightly, trying to be natural like he instructed. Except I'm not usually dripping wet as soon as I start, and I usually use my vibrator. I'm way too embarrassed to bring that up though, so I just keep rubbing myself like I think he wants me to.

"No," he says after a little time has passed. "I want to see how you do this when you're by yourself." He crosses his arms, watching me thoughtfully. "You use a toy, don't you? What is it. A vibrator? A dildo?"

I swallow my embarrassment down, trying to remind myself that he wants to know because it turns him on, not because he's trying to embarrass me.

"A vibrator," I say quietly.

The corner of his mouth pulls up. "My naughty little kitten. I fucking love it." He moves to a set of drawers behind him and rummages around until he pulls out a dildo a little smaller than the one I have at home with a vibrating attachment. He puts it in my hand and moves back to sit in a chair behind me, where he kicks his ankle onto his knee and leans back with a look of satisfaction.

He says nothing else, but I know I'm supposed to resume, so I close my eyes and try my hardest to pretend I'm by myself, even though I don't ever do this on my hands and knees. "I'm normally on my back," I say after a few seconds.

"On your back then," he says.

I roll over, spreading my legs out and using the head of the dildo to rub myself and spread my wetness across my entire pussy. I activate the vibrator and lean back, sucking in a deep breath as the pleasure begins to blossom from between my legs to the rest of my body. Knowing Damian's watching me has my sensations on overdrive, and when I look back up I see he's palming his erection, hand moving slowly as his eyebrows pull together in pleasure.

I nearly cum just at the sight of him getting off to me, but something tells me he wants me to wait. He's greedy when it comes to my orgasms, and I know he'll want me to cum around his cock. *I want that too.*

I dip the head of the dildo inside myself, taking my time with it more than I would if I was by myself, but I can hear how much Damian is enjoying the show. I drive it a little deeper each time, hips moving to meet each thrust until the clitoral stimulator is massaging my clit every time.

I want to watch Damian more, but the pleasure is getting so intense I can't keep my eyes open anymore. "Oh God," I gasp. "Oh fuck. I'm going to cum soon, I'm going too--"

"Stop," he says.

He stands up and takes the dildo from me. He runs his thumb along it, collecting my wetness and then he licks it off his finger with a smirk. "You're so fucking delicious."

My breath catches. The idea of him liking my *taste* is so vulgar in all the right ways, and I can't seem to get enough of it. I feel my walls still clenching around nothing and my clit throbbing. I need to cum so badly I'm not above begging him if he makes me.

"Now," he says. "Stand up."

I do as I'm told, even though my legs already feel a little weak.

He methodically removes my clothing, fingers brushing my bare skin where he can find excuses to and some places he can't. He gets me completely naked and then takes a step back to admire me with another half-smile. "Goddamn you are so fucking perfect."

I blush, folding my arms over my breasts self-consciously.

"No," he says, taking my arms and putting them back by my sides. "Don't ever cover yourself in front of me, Kitten. Do you understand? Your body is art to me. *You* are art. You wouldn't put a black box over the Mona Lisa and you wouldn't put a sheet over the statue of David. *And you will not cover your body in front of me.*

I bite my lip, nodding. If it's possible for words to change me from a self-conscious woman to one who's proud of her body, Damian is well on his way to doing it. I've never felt more beautiful or sexy than I do right now in this room, and losing the weight of doubt is freeing up more room for me to enjoy the pleasures of the flesh.

"You're going to take my clothes off with nothing but your mouth. And you're going to do it blindfolded," he adds.

He drapes a black cloth around my eyes and I'm left in total darkness, with only the sound of my own breathing for company. I inch forward, reaching blindly with my hands to find him but he makes a disapproving sound.

"No hands. Just your mouth."

I try not to think how ridiculous I must look scooting forward with my face extended slightly, but the sound of his voice gives me a pretty clear idea of where he stands. I bump into his chest a little roughly. I feel the lapel of his jacket with my lips. Taking it in my teeth and moving to slide it off his arms is easy enough, but the tie he wears is tricker.

He caresses me while I work at his clothes, pulling at the knot on his tie with my teeth as he strokes my breasts and back.

It takes me a minute to figure out the best technique for unbuttoning his shirt, but I eventually find a combination of tongue, teeth, and lips is the best method. When I reach the buttons near his stomach, I have to grip the shirt with my teeth and yank it free from his pants.

From the quick pace of his breathing, I can tell he's enjoying this.

I undo the last button of his shirt, and while I know I still need to tackle the cuffs on his sleeves, I'm too eager to get to his pants to worry about that right now. It only takes two or three quick yanks with my teeth to get his belt loose, and then the button at his waist. I take the zipper between my teeth, dragging it down slowly. His pants slide down on their own once I undo the zipper. I move my lips forward and immediately find the hard shape of his cock beneath his underwear. I tease him a little by moving my lips across its length until I find the tip, where a small spot of pre-cum is soaking through his underwear.

I bite my lip to hold in the wild urges coursing through me. Not bringing my hands up to touch him all over is almost impossible, but my desire to please him overcomes it. I want to be his good little submissive. *His little slut.* I want to be his dirty kitten-- the one he can't stop thinking about. I want his dick to get hard at the slightest thought of me, but above all I want to please him.

I take the waistband of his underwear in my teeth and yank it down to his mid-thigh. His hard cock springs free and presses against the side of my face. I turn my head so my lips graze the smooth skin of his length. His body quivers at the tender touch.

"Can I? Please, Sir?" I ask.

"Fuck..." he growls. I can hear the hesitation in his voice. He clearly had some kind of plan for me, but I'm tempting him to go off-script, and I love it. "You want my cock, Kitten?"

"Yes," I say. "Yes, Sir."

"You'll get it, but not for free. I want something too. Stand up."

I obey, standing so quickly my breasts bounce. That would normally make me self-conscious, but it instead gives me a small rush of excitement, because I know Damian is watching, and I know he is relishing in the sight of my naked body.

"You need to trust me now, but I won't drop you. Just relax."

I frown in confusion. I feel his shoulder press into my waist and his arms wrap around my ass. A second later, I'm flipped upside down with my breasts and thighs pressed tightly to Damian's body. He grips me firmly by the waist and pulls me up until I feel the scruff of his beard between my legs. It's only then I realize what he meant when he said he wanted something too. He meant if I was going to get to have his cock, he'd get my pussy.

"Can I use my hands?" I ask.

I hear the sound of his hand slapping my ass before I feel it. It rings out sharply in the room with a loud crack. A quick sting of heat follows that slowly blossoms outward with radiating pain.

"You will address me as Sir, or you will be punished."

"Yes, Sir," I say. The few times I've been slapped in the past have always brought out an irrational sort of anger, like I can go from polite librarian to Hell's Angels enforcer in a split second. The pain from Damian's slap has a similar effect, except it's somehow in a sexual context, like my already ridiculous lust was just kicked into overdrive.

"And yes, you may use your hands."

I wrap one arm around his thigh instinctively, even though his grip feels secure on my legs, I know if he let go of me I'd fall on my head right now. My other hand finds the thick base of his cock. Because of our height differences, it's a good thing his cock is so big, or I wouldn't be able to reach it with my mouth in this position.

I take the head of his cock inside my mouth. Even the tip of it is so wide it stretches my lips, but after the initial tinge of pain from the stretch, my lips adjust. I use the base of my tongue to cup him as I work my mouth up and down, swirling my tongue and dragging my bottom lip along the rim of his head.

My attention is yanked away from doing a good job on him when I feel the warmth of his own tongue plunge into me. He doesn't start slow. He *attacks* my pussy with his mouth, and it's several long seconds before I even remember I still have his cock in my mouth. I get back to work, subconsciously increasing the intensity of the blowjob I'm giving him as my own pleasure ramps up, which seems to drive *him* even further into a frenzy. The two of us feed off each other's lust, driving one another farther and faster until my hand must be a blur of motion along his shaft and my mouth is tingling from the friction of bobbing up and down on him.

I'm starting to feel heavy-headed from being upside down and straining so much, but the tingling pain that starts in my head and is building toward my neck is doing strange things to my body. It's like Damian said--the pain is acting like a reset button. Every time my brain registers the discomfort of blood rushing to my head, it's like the sensation of his tongue between my legs is hitting me for the first time again.

He starts to lap at me, driving his tongue inside me in wonderful ways while he uses his hand to give attention to every other inch of me. I jerk in his grip and nearly end up falling head-first on the ground when he pulls his tongue from my entrance and drags it up to the tight ring of my ass. I've never in my wildest dreams thought of wanting a man to put his tongue *there,* but a split second of Damian's attention has me completely re-thinking that. He starts plunging his fingers in my pussy even as he circles my ass with his tongue, probing the entrance and easing himself in a little bit at a time.

Somehow I'm still keeping enough focus on what I'm doing to keep sucking his cock, and I now have a cramping jaw and tired arm to add to the discomfort of blood rushing to my head. Instead of distracting me like I would expect, all the pain is only making his touch more explosive, like every nerve in my body is on full-alert and my synapses are firing on overdrive.

"Oh my God," I gasp, but my words come out as an unintelligible gurgle because my mouth is full of him.

I lose track of the line between just pleasure and mind-blowing orgasm. What normally feels like a clear-cut escalation blurs into feelings that never seem to fade or falter, like an orgasm without end. Every touch, every movement of his hands and mouth against me keeps the chain reaction going until I start to feel light headed and weak.

I don't know how long it is before he lets me back on my feet and eases me to sit on a padded table, but I sink backwards, panting and still moaning uncontrollably. He unties the blindfold from my eyes so I can see the satisfied expression on his face.

"You're doing amazing, Kitten."

"Thank you, Sir," I say breathlessly.

"Now, shall we begin?"

My heart falters. *Begin?* I thought we began a long time ago, but I nod, because more than anything, I want to please him.

The corner of his mouth pulls up. "That's good. Now, I know you feel weak right now," he says, moving to the far end of the room and giving me a wonderful view of his naked body. I guess he finished the job of undressing while I was blindfolded, and thank God for that. Every step he takes makes his ass flex and relax in a hypnotic way, and when he reaches for something on the wall, it makes his broad back cord and bulge in places I didn't even know muscles existed.

"Your body needs a reset," he explains, coming toward me

with a leather paddle. "You may have been uncomfortable, but the pleasant sensations were overpowering the unpleasant. You've overdosed on pleasure, in other words. Now it's time to reset the dial."

"You want me to overdose on pain?" I ask, feeling afraid for the first time.

"No. The pain doesn't need to be extreme, or even more than mildly uncomfortable. The point is that the pain comes by itself, devoid of pleasure. You may find an emotional release or even physical pleasure you won't expect in submitting to my punishment, but beyond that, this is how we prepare your body for the final act."

"The final act?" I ask.

"Now, now, Kitten," he says warningly. "I am allowing you certain graces because you are still not accustomed to being my submissive, but it's not your place to question me. I'm your dom. You need to trust that I will tell you as much as you need to know. I will do as much as I need to do. Remember, my ultimate goal is your pleasure. Beyond that, you just need to trust me."

I nod my head and close my eyes.

"Good. Very good," he says.

I feel the familiar surge of warmth from his praise. I realize how easily I could become addicted to pleasing him, but I also can't manage to figure out how that would be a bad thing.

"On your stomach," he says. "I want to see that beautiful ass of yours."

I roll over, noticing for the first time I'm on what looks a little bit like a massage chair. There's a recessed section where I can rest my forehead on a padded area and breathe easily while on my stomach, as well as pads that are set below the bench to rest my arms on comfortably.

"Now, I don't just punish you to enhance your pleasure. I'm also punishing you because you have displeased me over the course of the past few days. As my submissive, you need to learn that you may be afforded certain luxuries when we're not in settings like this, but if you overstep too far, even outside our playtime, you'll pay for it here. Remembering that will help keep you in line."

I clench my muscles tight, expecting him to hit me with the paddle at any moment. I'm afraid of the pain, but also excited in a way I can't explain. It feels like I'm diving deeper into this world of his, and with that dive comes a deeper commitment to him. The idea of tying myself more closely to him is as exciting as any of the pleasure he promises, because when I think of being with him now, I feel an overwhelming sense of safety, like as long as he's my dom and my lover, nothing bad can ever happen to me.

I feel myself finally giving my mind over to this experience one hundred percent. Up until now I've held back just a small part--the tiniest reserve of doubt that maybe this wasn't right for me, that a mother of a two-year-old had no business getting involved in something like this. But while it all feels dark and dirty in a sexual, thrilling kind of way, there's nothing actually *dark* about this, and even if there was, who says a mom can't have a dark side? If it makes me happy, then Dean will benefit more from my happiness than if I was repressing all my urges and unhappy.

The paddle collides with my ass harder than I expected. I jump up slightly, yelping with pain.

"Let the burn sink in," he says. "Commit the sensation to memory and remember it. *Use it.* Let it make you stronger."

I try to focus on the pain, mentally diving into the sensation until I can almost feel the outline of the paddle on my ass and the way little threads of discomfort spread from the spot, tingling and burning with gradually weakening intensity. He puts his hands into a small box at the foot of the bench and touches something before bringing them to my skin. He must have been touching something cold, because his hands are icy against me, immediately soothing away the sting of the paddle.

He repeats the process several more times, reminding me what I did to deserve each paddling before administering the punishment and soothing away the pain. By the time he's done, my ass is tingling and slightly numb, but the cream he applies takes away the last of the sting, leaving me with pain, only the memory and the vague tingle across the surface of my skin.

He helps me to flip over and sit up before lifting me. It looks like he's about to take me to another bench loaded with straps and harnesses, but I see from the look in his eyes we're not going to make it that far. I've never seen so much heat in a person's eyes as I see in his, and he lets out a low growl-like sound as he pushes me up against some kind of device with a vertical leather pad and horizontal metal bars overhead. My back is on the pad and my breasts are pinned between us.

Damian drives into me, lifting me off the ground and gripping my ass tightly. "I need you," he whispers. "I just want to fuck you. No more games. No more control. I want to let go and I want to fuck you until you're full of my cum."

I grip the back of his head with one hand and hold the bar over my head with the other, rubbing myself against him, searching for his cock with my body.

He pulls me down by the hips, sliding his length into me as he does. I cry out. My walls stretch to fit him, but the sensation is amazing, like a perfect fullness. He doesn't take his time getting every last inch of himself in me. He greedily pulls me down, filling me with more and more of his cock until my legs are forced apart by his hips and he's in me to the base.

"Oh God, you're so big," I gasp.

"You like that, Kitten?" he asks, working himself into me at a furious pace.

"Yes, Damian. Yes," I moan.

"Fuck," he roars. "You're so fucking tight."

I don't know how long it takes. I don't care. Everything falls away until it's just his body and mine moving together, like two dancers in the dark, completely in harmony. Every motion is like art and passion all blended together. When my orgasm comes, it crashes into me with the force of a tidal wave, threatening to undo me, but I cling to him, body quivering as he pounds his final thrusts into me and squeezes his eyes shut.

He lets out a groan of pleasure and his cock pulses inside me, filling me with the warmth of his cum. We stay that way for a while, joined together in the most intimate way, catching our breath while he holds me.

"Is it always going to be like this?" I ask after a while.

"No," he says. "It's going to get even better."

I smirk. "Now I know you're full of it. It can't be better than that. Nothing could."

"Remind me to punish you for doubting me next time. Maybe I'll paddle that pretty little ass of yours until you admit I was right."

"Sounds like a date."

14

EPILOGUE - DAMIAN

One Month Later

❧

"Did you see the box with my pots and pans anywhere, Kylie?" I shout down the hallway.

"No," she says. "But I did find your box of *trains*," she says with a mischievous grin. "I didn't see your conductor hat though, was that in another box?"

"A man needs to have hobbies," I say.

Her grin widens. "You just may have to fight with Dean over this hobby of yours, because, you know... He's two, and he likes trains too."

"You know you're going to pay for this, right?" I ask.

She bites her lip. "I was counting on it."

I'm about to pull her in for a kiss when Dean comes barreling through the new house on a little toy truck. He crashes into a wall and tips over. He looks to me and gives me a thumbs up and a smile before picking his truck up again and zooming off.

"He's going to love it here," says Kylie. "You know you didn't have to move, though. This is all so much, I don't know how--"

"Hey," I say, pulling her close and hugging her. "You're mine, Kylie. Mine to take care of. Mine to protect. Mine to love. That means you don't get to decide what is too much or what is excessive when it comes to me spending money on you. I want us to have this place together. And I want to make sure you have a chance to catch a breather whenever you need it," I say, drawing her attention to the front window, where we have a clear view of Angie arriving. "There's an in-law suite separate from the house where Angie will be staying. She's thrilled about the whole arrangement because she loves Dean and she loves you. Plus, she gets a free place to stay with salary and benefits."

"Damian..." she says. "I can't--"

"You can, and you will. You don't have to use her to watch Dean at all if you don't want, but she's here if you need her. So am I."

"I'm always going to need you," she says, gripping my shirt and standing on her tiptoes for a kiss.

"Damn right you are. Especially when we start filling this beautiful belly of yours with more babies."

A look crosses her face that makes me narrow my eyes, looking at her more closely.

She looks up at me with wide, searching eyes, then the shadow of a smile creeps across her lips. "I think we already started."

"You're pregnant?" I ask. "You're actually pregnant?" I can't help myself. I grab her by the hips and lift her up, spinning around a few times while I laugh. "We're going to have a fu--freaking baby!" I say, catching myself before I drop an "F" bomb within ear-shot of Dean.

Kylie laughs. "Not if you spin it out of me."

I carefully put her down. "I'm sorry, that was--"

"No. Don't be sorry. I was afraid you'd be upset for some

reason. We never talked about it, and I mean, now you're with a woman who has gotten pregnant *twice* out of wedlock. I thought maybe you'd think I was a hussy," she says, still smiling slightly but I can tell she was actually a little worried.

"There's nothing I want more in this world than being with you for the rest of my life and growing our family, Kylie. Nothing at all. Okay, there may be one thing."

She raises an eyebrow.

"Remember when you dropped your suitcase full of bathing suits three years ago?"

"Yes..." she says. "Are we playing the embarrassing memory game? Because this isn't going to be fair. All I have is the time you stubbed your toe and fell completely on your face."

I reach in my back pocket and pull out a post card. It shows a scene of a pristine beach in Bermuda and a rocky outcropping. "Look familiar?" I ask.

She snatches it from my hands, eyes wide. "You had this the whole time? I was looking for it when I got home and thought I lost it."

"It took me a little research and some time, but I found the place. I know we were going to get settled in today, but I went ahead and paid a team to handle the rest."

"You let us move half the boxes in the house and *then* paid a team to do the rest?"

I smirk. "I can't spoil you too much. Now you get the best of both worlds. The charm of working up a sweat on move-in day, and the luxury of knowing professionals are handling it all for you."

She grins. "So thoughtful."

"I thought so. Now go find Dean, because I've got a helicopter scheduled to pick us up in the back yard in about five minutes, and we can't go without our little man."

15

EPILOGUE - KYLIE

We land in Bermuda that same night on a dark runway in Damian's private plane. Damian surprised me by inviting Melina and Alec, who by some miracle are still dating, even though Melina usually cycles through boyfriends as often as most people change clothes. Angie came along too. There's even a man I've never seen before--he's about my height with a kind face and a mustache. My best guess puts him in his mid forties, and judging by the way he and Angie keep stealing glances at each other, I'm thinking Angie brought along a romantic partner too.

I smile to myself when I realize how important she has become to me over the past few weeks. I would've looked down on the idea of a nanny, because I thought it was just an excuse to neglect the kids, but I used to spend more time cleaning, cooking, and keeping up the house than I did focusing on Dean. Angie being here has given me so much more quality time with Dean than I ever could've had before, and it means I can sneak out of the house during his naps and at night without fear that he'll wake up while I'm gone, because I know Angie is there.

It's been perfect, like just about everything else since Damian came back into my life.

Damian insisted on a strict dress code of bathing suits for the flight, so we all look ready to go for a beach party as we descend the stairs from the plane. Angie, Melina, and myself all wear cover-ups over our swimsuits, while Damian, Alec, and Dean opted for board shorts and no shirts. I'm having trouble deciding between admiring how adorable Dean looks wearing a matching shorts to Damian's with his little belly hanging over the waist-band, or at how sinfully good Damian looks with his sculpted body on display. I eventually decide there's no problem in enjoying both.

Damian ushers us all into a limo, which takes us on a half-hour ride before we have to switch vehicles to a small convoy of jeeps that can handle a little bit rougher terrain. He has profes-sional drivers taking us through relatively dense forests that the drivers must know well, because it looks like we're driving straight into trees half the time, only to turn at the last second and take a hidden path.

We eventually break free of the trees to a view I never thought I'd actually see with my own eyes. It's lit by starlight instead of a blazing afternoon sun like in the postcard, but I'd know the scene anywhere. It's my beach. The beach I've spent half my adult life fantasizing about visiting, like coming here would somehow be a remedy for all that was wrong in my life. The irony is I only managed to make it here when my life is already fixed--when it's already perfect.

I squint down at the beach and notice tiki torches and some cloth tents set up a distance from the water. I also see a dozen or more people mulling about down there. I turn to Damian with a confused expression.

Except he's not standing. He's kneeling in front of me with both his hands raised up toward me. He's holding a diamond ring that catches the distant light of the torches and bounces it back in every color imaginable.

Everyone is standing around us in a semi-circle, watching with smiling faces, but they are just a blur to me right now. An engagement ring?

"Will you marry me?" he asks. Then he lowers his voice until only I can hear it. "Remember the consequences if you displease me." Damian winks.

My eyes well with tears of happiness. I fall down to my knees, forgetting the ring and hugging him so tight I don't know how he keeps from dropping it. I'm laughing and crying like a complete idiot, but I don't care.

"Well?" he asks after I've calmed down a little. "You're kind of leaving me hanging here."

"Yes," I say, taking his face in both my hands and kissing him. "Yes. A million times. Yes."

He slides the ring on my finger and grins at the sight of it. "Good. Because I would've had to explain to everyone down there why the wedding ceremony was canceled, and I brought them a long way to see this."

I frown in confusion. "Wedding ceremony? Isn't there usually the whole planning thing and--"

"Usually," he says. "But I couldn't wait. I'm sorry. I want it all. And I want it now."

I bite my lip, looking toward what I now realize is the place I'm going to get married. It's perfect.

"You're lucky I'm not one of those girls who spent her whole life fantasizing about my wedding," I say.

"Not lucky," he says. "I just did my research. I asked Melina. She said you always dreaded having to plan your own wedding because you hate making decisions. She said you also never cared much for traditional weddings with big dresses and suits and ties. What was it you said? It seems so stuck up and stuffy?"

I glare at Melina, who is studying the top of a nearby tree innocently.

"You knew?" I ask her.

She reluctantly looks back toward me. "Only for a few days. He made me promise not to say a word."

I shake my head, but I'm smiling. "Traitor."

"Well, they're all waiting for us," says Damian.

We all make our way down the somewhat steep slope of grass that eventually turns into pure white sand. I kick off my shoes so I can feel it between my toes.

"I've never felt sand this soft," I say.

Damian kicks his own shoes off and nods in approval. "Wow. Yeah."

Dean takes two steps before he face plants into the sand and sits up with a grumpy look on his face.

"This is *so* past his bedtime," I say with a laugh. "Are you sleepy, Deanie?"

"No," he says firmly. "Daddy. Hold," he stands up, reaching for Damian and yawns.

My heartbeat quickens when I realize he just called Damian daddy for the first time. I've spent some time with him trying to explain to him that Damian is his father, but at Dean's age, it can sometimes be hard to tell what's sinking in and what isn't. I wanted it to be a surprise for Damian, who thought we were still waiting for the right time to tell Dean. As far as I was concerned, the right time was right away, because I couldn't wait.

Damian kneels down and wraps his arms around Dean. At first, I think it's a trick of the light when I see something catch the light and slide down Damian's cheek as he squeezes his eyes shut and hugs Dean, but it's no trick. I feel my own eyes watering and I move in to hug both of them. *My little family.*

And my little family is going to keep growing if Damian has his way. Not that I'm complaining. Not in the slightest.

ALSO BY PENELOPE BLOOM

Thanks for reading Knocked Up by the Dom! Don't forget to join my mailing list if you haven't already! (You'll get a free book just for signing up!) Find all my books as well as a link to join my mailing list through Facebook or by searching my name on Amazon.com!

xoxo,
Penelope

More by Penelope Bloom
(The Citrione Crime Family)
His (Book 1)
Mine (Book 2)
Dark (Book 3)
Punished (*Amazon top 40 Best Selling Novel for February* Standalone BDSM Romance)
Single Dad Next Door (*Amazon top 12 Best Selling Novel for February*)
The Dom's Virgin (*Amazon top 22 Best Selling Novel for March)

Punished by the Prince (*Amazon top 28 Best Selling Novel for June)

Single Dad's Virgin (*Amazon top 10 Best Selling Novel for April)

Single Dad's Hostage (*Amazon top 40 Best Selling Novel for May)

The Bodyguard

Miss Matchmaker

54822122R00090

Made in the USA
San Bernardino, CA
24 October 2017